MISRULE MY HEART

A Tudor Christmas Romance

Rebecca Paulinyi

Copyright © 2021 Rebecca Paulinyi

All rights reserved

This is a work of fiction. Names, characters, businesses, places, events and incidents are either the products of the author's imagination or used in a fictitious manner. Any resemblance to actual persons, living or dead, or actual events is purely coincidental.

No part of this book may be reproduced, or stored in a retrieval system, or transmitted in any form or by any means, electronic, mechanical, photocopying, recording, or otherwise, without express written permission of the publisher.

Cover design by: GM Book Covers

For everyone who finds Christmas truly magical - no matter how old they get.

CONTENTS

Title Page
Copyright
Dedication
CHAPTER ONE											1
CHAPTER TWO											6
CHAPTER THREE										12
CHAPTER FOUR										28
CHAPTER FIVE										31
CHAPTER SIX											33
CHAPTER SEVEN										35
CHAPTER EIGHT										44
CHAPTER NINE										46
CHAPTER TEN											50
CHAPTER ELEVEN										53
CHAPTER TWELVE										60
CHAPTER THIRTEEN									65
CHAPTER FOURTEEN									77

CHAPTER FIFTEEN	82
CHAPTER SIXTEEN	84
CHAPTER SEVENTEEN	86
CHAPTER EIGHTEEN	90
CHAPTER NINETEEN	94
CHAPTER TWENTY	98
CHAPTER TWENTY-ONE	100
CHAPTER TWENTY-TWO	107
CHAPTER TWENTY-THREE	110
CHAPTER TWENTY-FOUR	115
CHAPTER TWENTY-FIVE	122
CHAPTER TWENTY-SIX	125
CHAPTER TWENTY-SEVEN	126
CHAPTER TWENTY-EIGHT	131
CHAPTER TWENTY-NINE	133
CHAPTER THIRTY	141
CHAPTER THIRTY-ONE	144
CHAPTER THIRTY-TWO	150
CHAPTER THIRTY-THREE	155
CHAPTER THIRTY-FOUR	164
CHAPTER THIRTY-FIVE	170
CHAPTER THIRTY-SIX	176
CHAPTER THIRTY-SEVEN	178
CHAPTER THIRTY-EIGHT	184

CHAPTER THIRTY-NINE	188
CHAPTER FORTY	195
CHAPTER FORTY-ONE	197
CHAPTER FORTY-TWO	211
CHAPTER FORTY-THREE	217
CHAPTER FORTY-FOUR	229
CHAPTER FORTY-FIVE	232
CHAPTER FORTY-SIX	234
CHAPTER FORTY-SEVEN	235
Want More?	241
Saving Grace's Heart	243
Afterword	249
Books In This Series	251
Books By This Author	259

CHAPTER ONE
Isabel

The flowers on the spinning wheel were fairly ceremonial; it had been a long time since I had seen mother sit and spin anything at it. But traditions were traditions, and since work was forbidden betwixt Christmas Eve and Epiphany, it looked well to have anything that could be construed as a work tool taken out of action - no matter that we were a family of money now, and had very little need of manual work.

I ran my hand across the blooms and smiled; tonight there would be yet another fish supper, and midnight mass, and then the festivities would truly begin. I had always loved the festive season, but since Father had begun to make his way in the world, everything had grown more sumptuous. The gowns, the decorations, the feasts planned for the revels… all so much more than I had grown up with.

There was even talk that by next year we might be invited to court to celebrate the season, with

King Henry, his Queen and all the other fine lords and ladies of the land. Wouldn't that be a sight!

This year, however, we were at home, and for that I was quite grateful. At eighteen, I was the last of the women I knew to not be betrothed - but then, before my father's business flourished so spectacularly, there had been no pressing need for me to be married. There had been boys I liked the look of, certainly - but no-one I'd had thoughts of marrying.

I had thought I would have some say in the matter, but things were different now. Yes the clothes were finer, the food was richer, the house was larger and warmer - but my options had also been limited.

As I walked through the great hall, which was busy with servants sweeping out the magnificent fireplace, ready for the yule log which would be selected later in the day - I tried to turn my thoughts around. No, many doors had been opened to me by Father's success at supplying the palace with silk, and losing any freedom I had to choose whom I might marry was a price well worth paying.

So I was pleased to be spending this Christmas with my family and the many guests we were opening our doors to - because if things went according to plan, I would be married by next year.

Married. It sent a thrill down my spine whenever I thought of it, although I wasn't too sure whether that was from excitement or fear. Or a healthy mix of the two.

I had not yet met the man whom my father was hoping to link me to; but I knew he was very much aiming to have us betrothed before Twelfth Night. A formal wedding could follow later; once we were betrothed, there would be no putting us asunder, and the man in question was to be one of the guests at the frivolities of the season.

I knew only three things of him: that he was a northern lord, with a large estate somewhere near Manchester; that he was twenty-five years my senior; and that he had three sons with his first wife, who had passed away the previous year.

"Sorry miss," a young serving girl ducked out of my way, looking downward and scurrying towards the stairs. We had never been properly poor, but the most we'd had was a cook and a maid, and so the increase in the number of staff was something I was having to get used to. I wasn't very good at staying out of the way when I was meant to - like now, when they were trying to prepare the room for the yuletide celebrations.

Standing by a small window in the stone facade, I looked out to the stables. Riding was simpler when were so much less important too - and, I supposed, because I was younger. Although I still wore my hair loose down my back, I was old enough now to know riding astride a horse, or unaccompanied, was unacceptable - as much as I had got away with it in the past.

"Isabel!" my mother called from the end of the corridor.

"Yes Mother?"

"Our guests will be here in less than two hours! You must make sure you are ready. You know how important it is to make the best first impression on Lord Lisle."

I ducked my head; "Yes mother." I knew a dress of red brocade was laid out on the bed for me, and that my simple day dress would not be acceptable to greet the important guests. Most were not lords and ladies, for they were at court or hosting their own festivities - but the man my father hoped to make my husband was most definitely high born.

Mother touched her hand to the side of my cheek, and smiled. "You are a pretty girl," she said. "But you know we must dazzle him so the issue of your birth disappears. Imagine being addressed as 'my lady' - what an honour you would bestow on this family."

I smiled up at my mother, whose hair still retained its blonde glow despite some grey beginning to appear. My mother, I knew, had married for love, despite neither of them having much money to bring to such a marriage - but she wished for so much more for me, and I was well aware of the duty I had to fulfill to help my family reach the higher echelons of society. With no brothers, just a sister, everything fell to me - and I would not disappoint my family.

"I'll go and get dressed," I told her, waiting until I was out of sight to take the steps two at a time. Perhaps, I thought, Lord Lisle would have a wonderful personality, and the age difference would not be too apparent; after all, I liked to think of myself as mature, even if I was young in years.

And to be a lady… that certainly was an exciting, scary prospect.

CHAPTER TWO

Avery

I had been to a fair few fancy houses since I had started working for the Viscount, but this was definitely one of the nicest. Apparently the family had only been occupying it a year - he had overhead the Viscount sneering that their money was made in trade - but it hadn't stopped him accepting the invitation to spend Christmas when one had not been forthcoming from the court.

Privately, the staff had felt that Viscount Purbeck had shown too much public sympathy to Queen Anne - who was very much falling out of favour with his Majesty - and that was why an invite had not been sent this year.

However judgmental my lord and master was about the way this family had come into their money, he wasn't going to turn down the invitation. If he were being honest - although I doubted he ever was - he would admit that he no longer had the money to celebrate the season in such a lavish way as he would desire. A title, yes, but precious few funds - and being out of favour with the King was not going to help matters.

Even in the North, rumours had reached us about the King's flirtation with Mistress Jane Seymour - and how he still hoped for a living son and heir.

"You there - are you going to stand out here all evening? There's plenty of work to be done."

I shook my head and disappeared into the stables, not sure who had noticed me letting my mind wander where it should not have been, but knowing I needed to make sure there was no cause for complaint about my work. For a boy who had lived on the streets for many years, the position of head groom of the stables for a Viscount was a grand step up - even if he didn't always manage to pay us every month. Still, I needed him to think I did a good job - if I ever wanted to move up further in society. People like those in this house made me hope it was possible; they'd not come from as low as me, of course, but they had been merchants and now were living in a grand house with Viscounts and Lords coming for the festive period. That was a jump in society all right - and it gave me hope I could go further.

I began to rub down the horses we'd brought with us. Four had pulled the carriage, and they needed much tending to. I spoke softly to them as I prepared them for the night, feeding them a carrot each I had brought with me to ease them into their new surroundings. The fifth horse was the most impressive. Shadow, his name was, and he was a magnificent black beast. Sixteen hands and as fast as the wind - and the Viscount's pride and joy. He was a great enthusiast when it came to horseflesh, and he brought Shadow everywhere, even if he no longer always rode him cross-country himself. No, I had been the one riding him today, and although that meant I had been exposed to the harsh winter elements, I loved the freedom of being able to travel at my own speed and with my own company.

It boded well that the Viscount had brought me along for the Yuletide journey, and that he trusted me with Shadow. When I did decide what my next step in the world was, I hoped he would give me a good reference - for I had learned that who you knew made a great difference in this world.

"It's all right," I told Shadow as I brushed down his sleek coat and let him take the carrot from my hand. He was wasted on the aging Viscount, really; he could cover ground at an impressive rate, as I had proved that day, and he enjoyed the challenge of jumping fallen trees, deep rivers and fences.

As I murmured soothing words to him and wondered where I would be sleeping that night, I heard the stable door open. Instead of making my presence known, I continued to brush Shadow, but did so from the darkness of the stall that was his for the night. If I could avoid being dragged into other chores I would; I knew no-one here, and the two servants that had been brought from home mistrusted me because they knew nothing of my background.

I had worked hard to keep it that way.

Although I was hidden, I could just see past Shadow's long neck, and I was surprised to see a woman enter. Not just any woman; she was clearly a member of the elite, with golden hair that cascaded down her back like a waterfall and a deep red dress that did not look like it belonged anywhere near a stable.

"Hello, Snowflake," she said, stroking the velvety nose of a grey palfrey that stood two stalls down from where I was hidden. "I'm sorry I can't ride today." The horse whinnied, almost as if it understood her sentiments, and I stood on tiptoes to see over the wooden slats.

She was beautiful, and she looked like she did not belong here, in my world.

"I'll try tomorrow, early," she promised, tickling the horse between the ears with a smile on her face. Her cheeks were pink from the cold outside and I wished I could see her eyes to check whether they were the enchanting blue I was imagining. "I don't think the lords and ladies will be up as early, so I should be able to escape." She sighed, then fed the horse something from her hand before drawing away. "Not that I should be saying any of that! It's a good job you can't tell anyone, Snowy."

And then she turned, and I almost fell into a pile of straw as I tried to watch her leave. What was it about her that caught my eye? I couldn't say. She was beautiful, beyond anything I had ever seen before - but it wasn't just that. It was seeing such beauty in the stables, seeing someone so highborn chatting away to her horse like it was something she did everyday.

Which, I would wager she did.

For several minutes I stood and stared at the point where she'd disappeared through the stable door - and then I was spotted. This time, not by a mysterious beauty, but by an older member of staff who had a kindly smile.

"We're bringing the yule log in, lad," he said, jerking his head in the direction of the woods. "Could you help us?"

"Of course," I said, following him from the stable with my own silent promise to the horses to return. It was a polite request, and I was rather curious to see the inside of the house, and their preparations for the festivities.

I most certainly did not need to think any more

about the woman. She was far above me, in station and beauty, and I had a plan. A plan to get ahead in this world, so that if I did marry, and if I were to have children, they would never end up on the streets like I had.

I wanted better - for myself, for my future, and for my descendants. And daydreaming about some lady - or duchess, or marquess, or whatever she may be - was not going to help me get there.

Even if her image would be there every time my eyes closed.

CHAPTER THREE

Isabel

The few stolen moments I'd had with my horse, Snowflake, had calmed my nerves. It was amazing how much an animal could understand me - and how talking to her made me feel I had shared the troubles I felt, even though I could not voice them aloud to anyone.

I was ready.

Hettie, the maid who had once been our nanny, had brushed and fashioned my hair until it shone, leaving it loose down my back save for a few intricate plaits around my crown. As I'd seen myself in the looking glass, I had wondered whether this would be the last grand occasion where I could wear my hair down; once I was married, veils and hoods would be the order of the day.

"Isabel!" My sister Grace bounded over. At sixteen she had not quite learned to control her excitement - although I believed that was thanks to her nature. It certainly was not for lack of trying on mother's part. But then it had only been in the last few years that anyone really cared about the deportment of two merchant's daughters, and so perhaps she would learn in due course.

"Isn't it wonderful!" she exclaimed, whirling around to look at the great hall, decorated with all manner of greenery. Hanging from the rafters was a kissing bough, which I had seen Grace making alongside Hettie the previous day.

I smiled; "It is - but you must calm down a little! Our guests will be here soon, in time for dinner."

Grace pulled a face that my father would have called unladylike. "Fish - again."

"Feasting will begin tomorrow, you know that - it's not so different than before, even if we are in a much grander house now!"

"Excuse me!" The sound of many heavy footsteps had preceded the shout, and we both jumped out of the way as six men carried the yule log through the great hall. It was enormous, and somehow indoors looked even larger than when we had gone out together as a family to select it. I could spot the ribbons I had tied on it - yellow ones that I no longer felt suited my hair - as well as those of my sister, mother and father. It had been a glorious day, and made me feel a little nostalgic for simpler times, when we celebrated as a family, perhaps with an aunt or uncle staying, but certainly not members of the nobility.

Those were thoughts I was trying to push away; this was an honour. And I was excited to be welcoming these guests - I had to remind myself of that.

Four of the men I recognised - our own staff, who worked on the land or serving my father - but two were new. I had not realised any of our guests had arrived, but if their staff were here, they must have - perhaps that was where mother and father were. I watched as the youngest of them, a man probably only a year or two older than I, checked the log was firmly in the fireplace before turning to leave.

Something stopped him, but I wasn't sure what - I was too distracted. His dark hair shimmered a little in the dying light of the day, and fell to near his shoulders. His clothes were simple, and did not look like they would keep him warm enough if he were working outside, but it was something about his eyes that distracted me. They were a dark brown, like smouldering chestnuts in the fireplace, and they were looking at me in a way no-one had ever looked at me before.

The moment was over before it had even begun, and I stood, a little shaken by the strange feeling that had touched me as our eyes had met. I had seen beautiful men before - although none, I'd wager, as beautiful as him - and never before had I felt whatever *this* was.

He followed the rest of the men out, stopping as he reached the door to pick up a ribbon that must have come loose. He bent to retrieve it - yellow, of course - and turned it over in his fingers once, twice, before looking round the room.

We were the only ones left, save the maid brushing away the twigs that had been dropped, and in three strides he was before us.

"My lady," he said, a polite bow of the head, before reaching out and holding the ribbon in front of me. I put out my hand and he dropped it into my waiting palm, so close and yet not quite touching me. Of course, that would not have been appropriate - but there was something so tempting that I almost closed the gap - almost.

"Thank you." I finally managed to force some words out, afraid he would think me simple if I stood there staring at him any longer, and he smiled, nodding his head once more.

"Oh look!" my sister gasped, far too excitable as usual, and as I dragged my eyes from his to see what she had spotted, I saw she was pointing to the ceiling.

"You're beneath the kissing bough!"

I laughed, nervously. It was an old tradition; whomever met below the kissing bough was to kiss and remove a berry. I had always found it amusing... but now, with my sister, a maid and this man before me, suddenly my mouth was bone dry and the whole affair not quite so amusing.

"Shush, Grace," I said, but he was already looking up at the ceiling, and I felt my fate was sealed.

"It would be terrible bad luck not to kiss beneath a kissing bough," Grace exclaimed, and I wanted to kick her and hug her in equal measure.

"Well," his voice was deep and smooth, and I felt my heart stutter slightly. "I wouldn't want to bring bad luck to the house at the beginning of the festive celebrations."

Before I had time to even consider his words, he had taken a step forward and, without any other part of his body touching me, his lips had pressed against mine.

I had been kissed twice before, by men who certainly would have taken greater liberties if they had been able - but never had my body responded like this. The kiss was chaste, but my brain felt as though it had evaporated into thin air, and a warmth spread through me that made me feel reckless and excited.

"Isabel?" My father's voice, from the hallway, and this beautiful, mysterious man jumped backwards, putting an appropriate amount of distance between us.

Father entered the room and all I could do was hope beyond hope that my red cheeks and lips did not tell the truth of all that had happened here.

It was not the kiss that was the issue; it was how I had felt.

He bowed his head once more and left the room, with only Grace and I - and possibly a maid - with any knowledge of what had just happened.

"Grace, you're here too. You look splendid, daughters - you must come now. Viscount Purbeck has arrived and been shown to his room, and I believe Lord Lisle's carriage is pulling up now."

I was glad his enthusiasm meant he did not require a response; I mutely followed, wondering when I would be able to think straight enough to speak once more.

Behind me, Grace skipped along in her yellow dress, giggling to herself. I knew her teasing would be something I would have to deal with this evening.

After I had met the man I was supposed to be marrying.

We stood near the doorway of the great hall, my sister and I, waiting for our father to make introductions. Grace didn't seem nervous, but then she wasn't about to be introduced to the man she would share the rest of her life with. The man she would have to share her bed with…

That was far too much to contemplate in company, and so I focussed on listening to Mother in the hallway, talking pleasantly with whichever gentlemen had arrived. I felt confident I looked the part in my red dress - the finest I had ever owned - with its cream kirtle that set off my complexion. I had been much more careful this summer to stay out of the sunshine, even when riding my beloved Snowflake, and mother had complimented my doing so.

Next to me, Grace stood tapping one foot every-so-slightly, a sign she was excited. Her yellow dress was also very fine, but we had both been told how important it was for me to make the right first impression on Lord Lisle. My gown was more expensive - but luckily, Grace understood why.

The first man to enter looked to be far older than the forty-four years I'd been told Lord Lisle was. He walked with a slight limp and his hair was entirely grey.

I hoped fiercely that this was not the man I was expected to marry - all while trying not to let those feelings show on my face.

"And these are my daughters, Isabel and Grace," Father said, gesturing to them as they performed a low curtsy that had been perfected over many years of finishing lessons. "Girls, this is Viscount Purbeck."

"It is a pleasure to meet you," I said, knowing that was what was expected of me while at the same time feeling relief coursing through my body. I could not imagine myself tied to such an elderly man for the rest of my life… no matter how high a position I might achieve.

I knew how important it was to raise our social standing with something more valued and enduring than money - and my marriage was the answer to those problems.

"Lord Lisle," my father said, and my eyes darted back to the doorway to catch the first glimpse of this man who, if my father had his way, would be my betrothed in the coming days. "I'd like to introduce my daughters - Isabel and Grace."

Another low bow - and my heart dropped almost as low as my head.

In my dreams, I had hoped for someone still with some semblance of good looks, even though I knew that Lord Lisle was many years my senior.

And I knew that looks were not the most important thing in the world - but there was no disguising the fact that Lord Lisle was much older than me, and long past his prime. He was overweight, leaving the buttons of his doublet straining to close, and as he smiled I could see the yellowing of his teeth and the balding of his hair.

I did not want to be shallow, but if it had been hard that morning to imagine myself with a husband, to imagine myself married to this man before me was unthinkable.

And yet, as I knew so well, it was my duty.

He took my hand and brought it to his lips, and I tried very hard to look pleased by his attention. This was what we wanted - as a family, this was what we needed.

So why did the young man with the beautiful brown eyes keep appearing in my mind?

Dinner seemed to take an age that evening. There were to be no games or dancing afterwards, as we were still in the advent period, so the true celebrations would start tomorrow - and for that, I was glad. I needed some time to be alone with my thoughts, for it was too difficult to process everything and keep a polite smile on my face, as well as finding answers for every comment thrown my way by our guests.

The Viscount, who I had met, was a widower, and Lord Lisle was obviously single too. The other guests were all couples or families: a merchant who had made his way in the world like father had, and his wife; Lord Tilbury, who owned the manor closest to ours, and his wife; and finally Mister Laxton and his wife and daughter. He was a yeoman father from the neighbouring town, but he did not seem flustered by dining with a viscount. Their daughter was, I thought, a similar age to Grace - and, they said proudly, the only one of six daughters who remained unmarried.

I was sure they thought I was very old to still be unbetrothed - but then they were unaware of my father's plans.

"So, Isabel," Lord Lisle said, turning to me as he took a great mouthful of wine. "How are you finding life here in Fountain House?"

I saw my sister out of the corner of my eye, as she forced down a bite of fish with a grimace on her face.

"It's lovely," I answered. "We've been here almost a year, but I feel I find some new part to explore every day."

"Exploring!" he said with a laugh. "Do you spend much of the day exploring?"

The truth was yes - but I knew that was not the answer he was in search of. I smiled, demurely I hoped, and shook my head. "My lady mother keeps me very busy," I said. "Needlework, lute dancing - my days are quite full!"

He smiled at that, his cheeks reddening from his intake of wine, and nodded. "All good pursuits, of course. And yes, it is a charming little house."

Little? I could hear the condescension in his voice. We may not have been titled, but I knew from visiting local families that Fountain House could match many homes of Lords and Ladies when it came to size - and I was also well aware that one of the reasons Lord Lisle was believed to be amenable to a match with someone below his social class was thanks to a lack of funds.

I may not have had a title, but I did have a considerable dowry - and that was enough to sway many a gentleman's head.

"Is your home very large?" I asked, sure of the answer but presuming that, like most men, he would be happy to brag about his assets.

"Indeed," he said, a mouthful of bread slowing him down somewhat. "The gardens are vast, and beautiful in the summer. And there are ten bed-chambers, and room for a staff of fifty…"

Which he did not need and could not pay for, I thought, before reminding myself to not be so uncharitable. My hot-headedness, my mother had always warned me, would be my downfall - and if my future was with this man, I needed to learn to hold my thoughts.

I remembered he was speaking and managed to smile in the right places. "It sounds wonderful."

"Of course, it's missing a woman's touch," he said, and I noticed herbs stuck between his teeth. "My sons and I get on all right, but when it comes to redecorating, or employing new maids - well, things just aren't the same without a female involved."

He was trying to flatter me, in return, I realised - and I tried so hard to look pleased at his words. Mother and Father were smiling at the top of the table, clearly encouraged by our conversation, and I needed to start on the right foot with Lord Lisle. There was no use daydreaming; I was an adult now, and this was my future.

"Well, my lord, I hope you find the right woman to do so soon," I said, and he smiled and reached over to pat my hand.

I wasn't expecting his touch - so forward, even in company - but I managed to stop myself from pulling away.

"I think that is very likely," he said and I knew, sadly, that we were both on the same page.

The yule log had been lit with the ashes of last year's log, that had been saved from the far more modest fireplace in our London townhouse, where we had lived so happily before we had been elevated to a position where we could own a manor such as Fountain House.

Midnight Mass had been held in the small chapel, which was not usually so full of guests, and we had finally taken to our beds, ready to rest in preparation for the celebration of Christ's birth.

But rest would not come to me. I let Hettie help me remove my dress and corset, unplait my hair and brush it for bed, and then I sat cross-legged on the four-poster, hoping I could bring some calm and order to my thoughts.

Every time Lord Lisle had looked at me, I had felt a shiver of panic go through me. Panic at the thought of tying my life to his, of being his to command, of sharing a home and a table and a bed with him.

And yet my mother and father had looked at me with such hope in their eyes, that I knew I couldn't voice my feelings. Ultimately, it was my father's decision whom I married - and then the decisions would be my husband's.

Just as I was feeling rather woeful at that thought, there was a light tap at door, before it opened and Grace slipped through.

"Grace!" I said. "We've got important guests! You definitely should not be roaming the hallways in your nightgown."

She rolled her eyes at me and gave a shrug. "No-one saw me," she said, and sat herself down on the bed next to me without an invite. "And I needed to talk to you. You're not going to marry that old Lord, are you?"

"If mother and father say I am, then yes, I am," I said primly. Grace needed a good influence - I worried she was not calming down as she grew older.

"Issy, you can't! He's so old, and he's fat, and he has horrible table manners, and he-"

"Grace!" I said, not wanting to hear this harsh list of his failings, which I had already been through many times in my own head. "You know how important it is that we marry well. Now father has money, marrying into titles is the only way we'll be able to move further up. Lord Lisle's father is a duke," I said, parroting words father had spoken to me days earlier. "I know he's a second son, but then so was our good King. He could be a duke one day - that's more important than looks, and youthfulness, and-"

"But that boy from the stable," Grace said, a dreamy look in her eyes and a smile on her face. "He was beautiful!"

"What boy?" I knew, of course I did, but I didn't want to give her the satisfaction of knowing that.

"The one who carried in the Yule log! The one who kissed you under the kissing bough!"

"Oh. Him." I hoped my cheeks were not as red as they felt.

"I may be young," Grace said, more loudly than she really should considering the hour, "But there seemed to be something between you and he."

I scoffed; "He's some labourer, or servant of someone staying. Why, he might even work for Lord Lisle!" The more I protested, the more desperate I sounded, even to myself - but protest I must.

She couldn't know that all night, whenever I had looked at Lord Lisle, I had compared him with the man from the kissing bough. Those eyes, those cheek bones, the muscled frame and the youthful glint...

No-one could know that. I needed to forget that.

"He was very good looking," Grace pressed.

"Good looks aren't important."

"Aren't they?"

"Not in a husband," I said. "I must marry for the family - as must you."

Grace sighed then, and I wondered if I should have protected her a little from my harsh words. But she couldn't live in her dreamworld forever;

the day would come, and probably not too far in the future, when father would betroth her to some lord, or even higher - and she would be powerless to refuse.

    Just as I was.

CHAPTER FOUR

Avery

I should have been sleeping. Although no work would be taking place over the yule period, the animals still had to be tended to, and undoubtedly the party would wish to ride out at some point over the next few days.

I had never had trouble sleeping; as a boy, I had managed to sleep on the streets, despite the noise and the smell that surrounded me. As a servant, I had bedded down wherever I could and not woken when people stepped over me. Now, I often got to sleep alone - and at the Viscount's grand manor, even had a small room designated as a bedchamber, that was accessed through the stables.

Tonight, I had a pallet up high in the stables. I was quite happy sleeping near the horses; they usually calmed me, and I liked to know I could keep a close eye on them. It was fairly warm, high in the rafters, with straw around me and a thick woollen blanket - but tonight, I could not sleep.

I had not realised, when I had seen her earlier in

this very stable, that she was one of the mistresses of the house. But what I had known all along was that she was far, far above someone like me.

I had been enchanted by her from the second I saw her talking to that horse, her dress swaying behind her, that golden hair falling about her shoulders… and that was all before I had tasted the sweetness of her lips.

How had I ended up beneath a kissing bough with a fine lady? She might not have a title, but I knew this family were wealthy - far wealthier than my master, in spite of his title. It was things like that which the higher classes did not like about this new wave of merchants - but I had no issue with the competition in the world being levelled a little.

Unfortunately, it would not be lowered to my level. I turned for the fifth time in as many minutes, facing the wooden walls of the barn and wrapping the blanket tightly around myself. A wife had not really been part of my plans - although I supposed I had imagined one being on the scene someday. No, I had big plans to achieve before I could settle down - a ladder to climb. I would never be a lord, or a fancy gentleman, but I wanted to be my own master. A yeoman farmer, perhaps - I had always liked working with animals. I wanted my own home, however humble, and the freedom to make decisions about my life.

As a child I had nothing; I had always sworn that would not be the case once I was an adult.

As a man of no consequence, no-one would care who I married, unlike those of the higher classes. I sighed, and turned back to face the barn and the horses. I would make my way in the world, and then I would find a woman I truly loved, and I would marry her and live the quiet, settled life I had always dreamed of.

Daydreaming of the sweet kisses of a beautiful, rich girl was no use in that aim, and so I vowed to put her firmly from my mind.

CHAPTER FIVE
Isabel

I slipped quietly from the house at first light, desperate to feel the wind in my hair. I knew if I asked I would be told now was not the right time to ride - so I did not ask. Usually I was a fairly obedient daughter, but when I really set my heart on something, I tended to find a way to accomplish it.

No-one was awake, having gone back to their chambers to sleep after the first mass of the day, and I had left as early as I could without resorting to riding in the dark. That was one of the worst things about winter - waiting for the sun to rise in the mornings. I had always been an early riser, but living life by candlelight was never much fun.

If I had asked, I would also have been told I needed someone to accompany me - and that was another reason for slipping out unnoticed. As good-intentioned as the maids were, none of them could ride like I could - and this morning, with limited time, I just wanted to be free.

No-one cared so much about me having a chaperone when we had no money.

"Merry Christmas, Snowflake," I whispered, running my fingertips down her velvety nose. As she whinnied, her warm breath met the cold air in a cloud of steam, and I shivered. My thickest riding cloak was doing little to ward off the cold - but once we were out, I knew we'd be fine.

Quietly, I saddled her up, grateful for the years of self-sufficiency which meant I didn't need someone to do these tasks for me.

And then I was away, out of the stable door and onto the crisp, frost-covered ground. The bright blue skies and wintery air made me glad to be alive, and I turned Snowflake towards the woods, keen to gallop and canter and jump in this short burst of freedom, which might be my only for the next few days.

CHAPTER SIX
Avery

Despite how quiet she had been, I had woken as soon as I had heard her voice, wishing the horse a Merry Christmas. I smiled at that. She had said she would be back that morning; and I had hoped, in the back of my mind, that I would see her.

From high up in the hay, I watched her saddle the horse. I was itching to offer to help - it was what I did every day, after all. I wasn't used to watching fine young ladies saddling their own horses - but she had no idea I was there, and so I did not interrupt. She vaulted onto the horse and I watched, impressed, as she confidently head off into the snow-flecked grass. Her horse was, as befitted a lady, a fairly calm and dependable palfrey - but she certainly knew how to ride.

I watched as she set off at a pace towards the forest, wishing I could mount Shadow and follow her, watch her gracefully ride through the woods and rivers that this beautiful area would afford her. The fact that she was - scandalously - riding astride... well, that only impressed me more.

And then I saw, right on the horizon, the horse stop sharply and Isabel - for I'd heard her father say her name yesterday - tumble straight off her back.

I didn't think. Taking the ladder steps two at a time, I landed on my feet in the middle of the stable, vaulted onto Shadow bare-back and galloped towards her. He was a responsive ride, and luckily knew me well enough to trust me, as we headed out into the icy air.

CHAPTER SEVEN
Isabel

My head was pounding like someone was drumming in the distance, and there was a sharp pain in my side. I took a breath or two, trying to calm my racing heart and take stock of whether anything was seriously damaged. I had tumbled off a horse before, but not for a long time, and I had never fallen in such a bad way.

It was my own fault, I knew, and I looked round to check if Snowflake was all right, and still with me. I winced as my body moved, but she was there, eating grass and looking a lot calmer than I felt.

The patch of ice that was to blame was beneath my left foot, and I could feel the cold getting to me, along with the aching that was spreading through my body.

I had been an idiot to ride in icy conditions alone; I had pushed Snowflake too hard, for my own fun, and now nobody knew where I was. Would I be able to ride home? I wasn't sure, but the pain in my ankle suggested not for a while.

Then, suddenly, I heard the pounding of hooves. As much as it hurt my pride to be discovered like this, I felt an overwhelming sense of gratitude for whoever was out riding - because too long out here in the cold and I'd probably be ill until Twelfth Night. Let alone the trouble I would be in with my parents.

I twisted with a gasp, and blocked the winter sun from my eyes with one gloved hand to see who my rescuer was to be.

And then I lost my train of thought completely.

He was wearing tight breeches and a thin lawn shirt - certainly not suitable attire for the weather - and rode an impressive black stallion with no saddle. His black hair streamed behind him as he rode and, before he had come to a complete stop, he jumped off and was by my side.

My heart raced once more, this time not in panic. This was a very different sort of danger I was in...

"Are you hurt?" he asked, his voice clear despite the worry in his eyes.

I shook my head, struggling to find my voice, before realising that was a lie.

He bent down by my ankle and gently pressed

it, then looked up as I tried to hide a groan.

"Are you sure?"

"I don't know," I answered. "Everything aches…"

"You took quite a tumble," he said. "What happened?"

"We hit some ice," I said, trying to get myself into a more elegant position but failing. "Snowflake flailed, stopped and I went flying. I think she's all right…"

He glanced over to where she was munching grass. "She looks like it never happened. You, on the other hand…"

He looked me up and down and I blushed, feeling embarrassed at the state I must look. "If you could just help me up," I said, as primly as I could, "I can get back to the house before anyone misses me."

"Riding without anyone knowing where you're going does not seem like the wisest idea," he said, raising his eyebrows. I blushed again; no, it hadn't been, but I wasn't going to admit that to anyone

"Normally, I'm a perfectly competent rider," I said, reaching my hand up and hoping he would help me without further comment.

His hand was bare, and even through my gloves

I could feel his warmth. I wondered if he had a fever, although he looked perfectly healthy.

"Why are you riding at this time in the morning, with no saddle?" I asked, trying to fill the silence that buzzed between as as he helped me to my feet. I was proud of myself for not wincing visibly.

He shrugged, and looked away. "I saw you fall," he said. "I thought you might need help."

"Well, thank you," I said. "I would not have liked to have spent hours out here in the cold before someone found me."

He smiled then, and I felt my heart jump around erratically. It wasn't fair that he was so good looking; it wasn't fair that he could make me feel so good just by being close to me.

He shouldn't have been close to me - that was the problem.

"My pleasure," he said, still holding my hand. "Not the best way to start the Christmas festivities."

"Indeed - and I had better get back for Mass."

He nodded; "Can you ride?"

I gingerly took a step forward, and felt a throbbing in my foot. Hopefully it was sprained, and not broken - but I was not sure I could even get back on Snowflake.

"I don't think so," I admitted. "But I'm not sure how far I can walk, either."

He looked at me for a moment, clearly thinking, and I took the opportunity to just let myself get lost in those deep brown eyes, and think about how it would feel to touch the hair that threatened to fall into them...

"You'll have to ride," he said in the end. "It's too far to walk if you're in pain. I'll help you up, and lead the horse - does that sound all right?"

I nodded - there was no other option. I didn't feel safe riding alone; my head still throbbed, and if I passed out on the horse at least he would be there to catch me.

Whether his presence was making me more or less likely to faint was another question entirely.

I half-walked, half-limped towards Snowflake, who nuzzled me apologetically, then looked at him. His strong arms clearly would have no issue in lifting me - but it certainly was not appropriate.

"How-"

His fingers encircled my waist without a word, and he lifted me into the air until I could easily seat myself in the saddle. He didn't comment on the fact it was not a side saddle, and so I didn't mention it - but I did rearrange my skirts to make sure I was properly covered. As he took the reins, I held on to the pommel tightly and assessed the damage to my dress. It was not good; if I managed to sneak in the house without anyone noticing, it would need to be hidden at the back of my wardrobe, for the rips and grass stains would certainly raise unnecessary questions.

"Come," he called, and I turned my neck to see the glorious black horse following along behind.

"He's an impressive horse," I said, not wanting to be rude and ask whose he was.

"He belongs to the Viscount," the man said. It made sense; I had heard the Viscount liked to keep a well-stocked stable, although the fact that he was spending Christmas with us suggested his star was not in ascension with those at the top.

"Your employer?" I asked.

He nodded, and I wondered how to get him to talk. We made slow progress back towards the house, and I so desperately wanted to hear his rich voice again. I was trying to ignore how my waist tingled where he had held me to lift me, with little success.

"Can I ask your name, since you rescued me?" I asked, wanting to know more about this mysterious, handsome man who was somehow leading my horse.

"Avery, m'lady," he said, and somehow there was a distance between us that hadn't been there when he had found me on the floor. I was reminded of the social distance between us, and how I really should not be with him alone…

"You're a talented rider," I said, just wanting to continue to talk to him in this brief moment I would be allowed.

"Thank you," he said. There was a moment of silence, then he continued, and I felt my heart soar. "I learnt as a young boy - and I'm lucky now to be in charge of His Lordship's horses - including Shadow, who is an incredible specimen."

I nodded, although realised he was looking forwards, the house almost in sight. "He really is."

"You're a talented rider, too," he said.

I laughed; "When I'm not falling on ice!"

"I've never seen a lady saddle her own horse before."

I paused for a minute; I didn't realise he'd seen me. Had he been in barn? I hadn't thought anyone would be there, since all our staff slept in the kitchens or the great hall - but I hadn't thought of the staff brought by the other guests. I was about to ask him, when I heard a loud voice carrying over the quiet grounds.

"Isabel? Isabel!"

Avery froze, and I glanced around in panic. It was Father, and while I didn't think he'd seen me, he soon would.

"Quick!" I hissed. "I need to hide!"

He sprang into action, leading us behind a large bush. Shadow followed, and although we wouldn't escape a closer look, I hoped it would be enough to not tempt anyone to look in the forest.

I slid from the horse, wincing as my ankle hit the ground and wishing I'd asked Avery for help.

"Why are we hiding?" he asked in a whisper, offering me his arm to balance me.

I took it gratefully, hoping he wouldn't notice the affect he had on me. I blushed; "I shouldn't be out without my maid. If I get seen alone with you, in this state…"

He paused, and then grinned bashfully. "It would ruin your reputation?"

I sighed; "Something like that. I'm sorry…"

"Don't be," he said in a whisper. "No-one's ever worried about me ruining their daughter's reputation before. It's almost a compliment."

I laughed, very softly, hearing my name called again but further away. "I was stupid to come out alone on an icy day, and very lucky you came to rescue me." I turned and our faces were as close as they had been in the great hall, and I remembered feeling his lips against mine and the way it had warmed my whole body. For a few moments we stood there, neither speaking, and I wondered if he were thinking the same scandalous thoughts, thoughts that couldn't go anywhere...

But there was such a short distance between our lips...

CHAPTER EIGHT

Avery

She was a vision, torn dress or no, and I felt a burning desire coursing through me as I stood so close to her. I shouldn't have been here, I shouldn't have held her hand earlier, or lifted her onto her horse, or kissed her beneath the kissing bough...

But that didn't matter now. Somehow we were crouched behind a bush, and her lips were a whisper away from mine, and all I could think of, all I could dream of was kissing her once again. Kissing her where no-one could see, where I didn't have the eyes of her sister and her maid on me, where we could be just be man and woman, giving in to the feelings that threatened to consume us...

"Isabel!"

And then the spell was broken. Because she was not any woman, and I was not the man for her.

"I should go," she whispered, and we were close enough that I could feel her breath on my face. "I can limp from here. Would you mind taking Snowflake back for me, please?"

It had been a long time since someone had asked me to do something, and not just told me, and I couldn't stop myself reaching out and taking her gloved hand.

"Are you sure you'll be all right?"

She smiled, and nodded, and before I could think about it I lifted her hand and pressed my lips to the soft leather of her glove.

She blushed, and then turned to go. "Can you not mention this to anyone? Please?"

"It's our secret," I promised, and then I watched her go, wondering how on Earth she would manage to get in the house without someone seeing her. At least, I supposed, if she was alone, she could just claim to have fallen. No-one would suspect she had been ravished...

Heat flooded to my cheeks at the thought of that as I tried to focus on getting the horses back, and not daydreaming about Isabel.

A Merry Christmas indeed.

CHAPTER NINE

Isabel

I was so exhausted when we sat to break our fast as a family, alongside our guests, that I struggled not to yawn as Lord Lisle spoke to me. Somehow I had made it through the side door normally only used by servants, and limped a little up the stairs to my chamber. Only a boy from the stables had seen me, and when I'd asked him to send up my maid as quickly as possible, he'd hurried away - hopefully not to tell my parents.

Once I was appropriately attired, with the offending dress at the bottom of a chest until I could repair it, I had headed down to dine.

"Where have you been, Isabel?" my mother asked softly as I sat beside her. "When Grace came to find you, she said you were not in your room."

Father was looking over, concern and suspicion in his eyes, and I hoped my lie would sound convincing.

"I could not sleep after mass," I said. "So I

thought I would take some air. I'm sorry if I worried you."

"I shouted for you," Father said, although I doubted our guests could hear him, he spoke so quietly.

"I'm sorry, Father," I said, then turned to Lord Lisle. It effectively ended the conversation, and as long as no-one - aside from Avery, of course - had seen me on Snowflake, the story would hopefully hold up.

"Do you enjoy the festive celebrations, my lord?" I asked, and as he paused in his eating to answer me, I let my mind wander places it certainly had no business being.

◆ ◆ ◆

The big celebration would be later that evening, and I knew the servants - and Mother - had worked extremely hard to organise a feast that showcased our new status in life. There would be another mass, which I presumed Avery would attend, as was generally the case among the staff - but when everyone went to rest or wander the grounds, I decided I needed to thank him properly for his assistance this morning. I tried to convince myself it was so he wouldn't tell his master, but somehow I knew he would not; I just wanted to see him.

That was a dangerous thought... but it was perfectly appropriate for me to go to the stables, and perfectly likely he would be in there. Tending to the animals, after all, was not prohibited during the twelve days of Christmas...

On a whim, I went through the kitchens, where the servants were hard at work. They smiled, but didn't stop to ask me where I was going - after all, why should they? Without being noticed, I sneaked a hot mince pie from a tray and, on my way out of the door, decided to grab an old coat of Father's. He wouldn't notice it was gone, and it was far too cold for Avery to be out in this weather in the clothes he had been wearing - even if they had fitted him so very, very well.

A flurry of snow had fallen once again, and I picked my way through, feeling the cold slush around my feet. I was glad I had worn my thickest cloak, and wrapped it around myself to ward off the cold.

I entered the stables, checking to make sure no-one was in the direct vicinity to see me, and when he wasn't immediately obvious, called his name softly.

"Avery?"

He swung down from a ledge above the stalls, and I realised then that he must have slept there, and seen me leave this morning. Well, thank goodness; otherwise my tumble might have had disastrous consequences.

And I never would have felt his hands on my waist.

"Twice in one day!" he said, a smile on his lips, and I felt my words dry up and my heart stutter. He wore a cloak this time, although nothing like my fine velvet one, and his dark hair looked as black as a raven's wing.

CHAPTER TEN

Avery

I had not expected to see her alone again. I knew she would be in mass, which I would attend because it was expected of me - although I had to admit that all the singing and praying in Latin was a little beyond me. But there I might have seen the back of her dress, her loose hair down her back - although not the fine features of her face, or the way the colour rushed to her cheeks when she tried to speak to me.

I was not ashamed to admit that I knew I had an effect on her, even if she didn't want me to - or that she had a similar effect on me.

"These are for you," she finally said, handing me a thick coat and a mince pie. It was still warm, and the smell made my mouth water. Later there would be a feast for the servants, which they had kindly invited me to. Nothing as grand as for the guests, of course, but for us it would be the richest food we had eaten all year. I would have liked to have spent it with family, but alas, I had none, and so in a warm kitchen with friendly people was the best I could have wished for.

"Thank you," I said with a smile, touched at the thought that she'd gone out of her way to bring me something to keep me warm. The cold never really bothered me, but the gesture meant a lot; it was rare for anyone to care so much.

"Thank you," she said. "That's also why I came… I just wanted to say thank you, again."

"Are you feeling better?" I asked. She had obviously changed and held no external signs of the fall she had taken.

"A bit of a headache," she said. "But nothing too bad - thankfully."

"Did you get in trouble?"

She smiled then, and for a moment I felt like we were just two mischievous kids, trying not to get into trouble for some prank.

"Apparently I can be very deceptive, when I want to be!"

"I can imagine," I said, wondering how old she was. The fine clothes made her look more mature, but I guessed she was younger than me - and, by the fact that her hair was worn loose, I presumed unmarried.

I took a step towards her, feeling that pull that

I'd felt when she'd first walked into the stable yesterday, and she didn't move. Our eyes stayed locked, and as her chest rose and fell with each breath, I could see her breathing speed up, just as mine was.

It shouldn't have been there, but there was something between us neither of us could deny. Something that had not been satisfied by a chaste kiss beneath a kissing bough…

CHAPTER ELEVEN
Isabel

He broke the eye contact first, putting the coat and pie down on a hay bale. When he looked back up, my mind was still swirling, and although I knew I should leave, I did not have the will to.

An errant wisp of straw settled in my hair, and before I had a chance to remove it he reached forward to take it between his fingertips and ever so slowly dropped it to the ground. Yet his fingers lingered lightly at the ends of my long, golden hair, and he took a step towards me that I should have run from.

My feet did not move.

I had always done what I should, but right now my body was screaming for me to give in to this strange feeling that had overtaken me. I was too innocent to truly understand it, but I knew that I had never felt it before - and that it was certainly not inspired by Lord Lisle.

I took a step forward, not knowing why, and stood so close to him I could feel the heat of his body. There was a smile on his lips as he moved closer still, his hand moving from the ends of my hair to the base of my neck, causing me to gasp and his smile to become greater still.

With a hair's breadth between us, I knew he was going to kiss me again - and I was quite content to let him.

"Mistress Isabel?" a voice called from not too far away, and I jumped backwards, just as Avery did the same thing.

My eyes widened in shock as the call was repeated. "Mistress Isabel!"

"I must go!" I whispered, turning on my heel, but the voice was coming closer, and I knew to whom it belonged.

"He's coming here! You must go, please."

"Who is?" he asked, and although I did not have time I hurried an answer as I pressed the coat and pie back into his warm, strong hands.

"Lord Lisle," I said. "My parents plan to betroth us, and if he sees me with you…"

He nodded, although something flashed in his eyes that I didn't have time to fully comprehend.

Then he was gone, back up above the horses, and Lord Lisle's heavy footsteps were entering the stable.

"Mistress Isabel," he said, his face ruddy and a smile on his lips. "I heard you enjoyed riding, and thought I might find you in the stables."

I tried to smile, and hoped my beating heart would calm enough to not betray how close I'd been to kissing Avery; and how close I'd been to being discovered in such a position, and therefore ruined.

What a silly, silly risk to take.

"I do love to ride," I said, walking towards Lord Lisle, and away from Avery, away from the risk I had so nearly taken. "My horse, Snowflake, is over there."

He glanced in her direction, and then looked back at me. "Perhaps we can ride together, on St Stephen's day?"

I lowered my head in what I hoped was a modest way, although it was in part to stop him seeing the feelings I was sure my eyes betrayed.

"That would be lovely."

Such lies - but such necessary ones.

"I believe it will be time for Mass soon, and then for the feast to begin!" he said, and I was surprised at how quickly time had passed today. "Can I accompany you back to the house? I'm sure your father will be pleased to see us getting along."

The meaning behind that could not be ignored, but I tried to; until father officially broached the subject of us becoming betrothed, it would be forward of me to acknowledge it. And ignoring it made it seem less real, somehow...

"Thank you sir," I said, desperately trying to think of a reason for him to go on ahead. I needed to speak with Avery, to say goodbye properly after I had hurried him away, and to make absolutely sure he knew that there could be nothing between us.

Not even that kiss that I was so desperate for.

"Shall we?" he said, holding out his arm, and as I put my gloved hand in the crook of his elbow, I felt a shiver of distaste at being so close to him. We walked into the frosty sunlight, before I feigned forgetfulness.

"Oh! I nearly forgot, my sister asked me to collect some more holly for the kissing bough."

He smiled indulgently. "I can wait."

"No, my lord, it is far too cold. Please, go back inside - and perhaps we could play a game of cards later, when the festivities begin?"

"That would be lovely," he said. "Although I

warn you, I don't like to lose!"

'Neither do I,' I thought to myself, but left the unladylike words unspoken in my mind.

I gave him a moment to start heading towards the house, then pretended to search for holly, before darting back into the stable.

He was stood there, leaning against a post, the coat looking a little big on him but immeasurably warmer than his other clothes. He had taken a bite of the pie, and I watched for a moment as he licked his lips, both waiting for the other to speak.

In the end, his words were first, and they struck a note in my soul.

"You're going to marry *him*?"

I nodded, not sure what else to say; I didn't need to justify myself to a man in charge of the horses.

I didn't have much to say on the subject, anyway.

"Why?"

"Why not?" I asked, knowing there was a very long list in my own head against the match, but not feeling the need to share that with him.

"Because he's so much older than you? Because he has no interest in horses? Because he looks at you like - like-"

"Like what?"

He looked away, took a deep breath, and then shook his head. "Forgive me. I have overstepped."

I nodded, although I desperately wanted to know what the end of that sentence was. How did Lord Lisle look at me? I presumed not with the disdain I tried to hide when I looked at him.

"I will marry him because it is what my father wishes, and a daughter must obey her father. I will marry him because he is titled, and in need of a wife with a good dowry, and because he will improve the fortunes of my whole family."

I was getting angry now; how dare he question my motives, how dare he judge the match my father was trying to so hard to make? Who was he to think he knew better?

I took a step towards him, drawing myself to my full height, feeling the anger heating me despite the cold weather. "I do not have the luxury of choosing whom I marry."

"Unlike me?"

"Indeed."

"I can choose whom I marry - as long as she is not born too highly."

We stood awkwardly, the truths hanging in the air, each of us a prisoner to the expectations of our class.

My anger died. I knew how lucky I was - but I didn't feel so lucky when I looked at what my future held.

"I'm sorry, Avery," I said. "But I can't…" I can't what? I can't kiss you? I could not say those words aloud, even if they were true.

Even if I truly wanted him to know.

"I can't follow my own wishes," I said finally, avoiding the use of the word desires in case my face flamed even more crimson.

"Don't apologise," he said, a half smile on his face. "A kiss under the kissing bough was more than I ever expected."

I smiled, then on a whim pressed a kiss to his cheek. It was rough beneath my lips and smelled faintly of sandalwood and straw.

"Goodbye, Avery," I said, and left before I did anything I might later regret.

CHAPTER TWELVE

Avery

I watched her leave, still feeling the whisper of that kiss on my cheek. Her dress - a moss green today - disappeared round the stable door, and I felt my heart take a dive. What else could I do?

She was right - whatever spark seemed to have ignited between us when we had kissed beneath that kissing bough; which had ignited for me when she had come to these very stables and spoken with her horse - that spark would have to fade. Because she needed to marry for her family - even if it was to a man like Lord Lisle.

And I needed to focus on being promoted highly enough, on getting my own farm, so that the next time I felt like this about a woman, I would not have to walk away.

◆ ◆ ◆

I joined the staff that night for their Christmas feast, once the rest of the household had dined. I tried not to think what she would be doing, what she might be wearing, how that lord might contrive to stroke her hand, or steal a kiss...

Other than me, and a couple of personal servants to the visiting guests, the table was mostly filled with the staff who served here daily, and they were merry bunch. The food - leftovers mainly, from the feast upstairs, although the cook had hidden away some comfits that had never made their way from the kitchen - was delicious, and the fire burned cosily in the grate. There was beer and wine aplenty, and I found myself relaxing enough to enter into a game of cards with the kitchen maid, which she won, and a spirited discussion of horses with the gardener who doubled up as a groom.

"Unusual to bring along a groom," he said, looking me up and down.

"The Viscount takes riding very seriously," I said with a shrug. "He likes me to be with the horses wherever he takes them - and he heard there was likely to be good riding on St Stephen's Day."

"Oh, I should think so," he said, swigging his beer and grinning. "Even before the master had quite so much gold at his disposal - well, they always liked a good horse."

"Do the whole family like to ride?" I asked.

"The lady of the house not so much, nor Mistress Grace - but I don't think I've ever seen a lady ride so well as Mistress Isabel, and the master, well, he's always been a confident rider. I'm sure you've seen he has some impressive horses in the stables."

I nodded; they were fairly impressive, although nothing rivalled Shadow in any stable I had been to yet.

I tried not to think of her riding, of how in awe I'd been as she'd saddled her own horse and dashed off astride into the winter's morning.

They all seemed happy to be working there, and the cheer of the season spread to all of us. Carols were sung and much excitement was in the air as we discussed the ball that was to be held two nights hence, to celebrate the festive season and the lady of the house's birthday - which all the staff, and the local people, were invited to, as well as the guests staying and any local landowners. It would be a merry occasion indeed, and that was before the gift giving of New Year's Day.

It occurred to me as we talked that I still had not thought of a gift for the Viscount; it was, of course, customary for me to present him with a gift, and for him to present me with one in return. For all his curmudgeonly ways, he had been very generous the previous Christmas, gifting me a fine set of whittling knives. Perhaps I would whittle him something; I would ponder it tonight once I was abed.

"She's to marry him, I heard," an older maid was saying at the end of the table, and I found myself listening in to her conversation, although I tried to look like I was simply relaxing by the fire.

"Lord what's-his-face?" the cook was saying, her face screwed up in disbelief. "But he must be, what, thirty years older than her?"

"Something like that," the maid said. "He looks at her like he wants to eat her up."

Something was said then that I didn't quite catch, but I gathered it was bawdy by their laughter and the reddening of their cheeks.

"She's such a beautiful, sweet thing though," the cook said. "A little spoilt, perhaps, but to be married to a man so much older than she is, with nothing in common…"

"Aye, but he's a lord, isn't he! A second son, but his father's a duke, so there's always a chance…"

"You think they're shooting for a duchy?"

The maid shrugged. "I think she's just doing what she thinks is best for her family, from what I've heard her saying to Mistress Grace. But you know Mister Radcliffe has got high ambitions…"

CHAPTER THIRTEEN
Isabel

I was exhausted - from my ride, my fall, from putting on an act in front of all of the guests. From playing cards with Lord Lisle and managing to avoid his fingers lingering on my hand as they so clearly were attempting to do. I was so full of food, and wine, and confusion as to why it was so hard to forget a man in a stable who I was so ready to kiss...

And yet sleep evaded me.

I did try. I tried to put his face from my mind, tried to not imagine what it would have been like to kiss him properly, in ways I could barely even imagine through my own lack of experience - but he filled my thoughts in a way that I had never known.

Would Lord Lisle ever fill my thoughts like this? I struggled to imagine he would - but then I knew my marriage was not meant to be for love, or romance, but for progression, for money, for continuing on a family line that was worth more than the one that came before it.

I would not think on him. Once Twelfth Night had been and gone, I would never see the handsome Avery again - and then I would be a wife, and perhaps by next Christmas a mother. My life was on the precipice of such big change, and I knew I could not afford to let my girlish fancies run away with me.

I must keep my eye on the prize: my family at court, my sister making an enviable match, the pride my parents would feel as their standing increased in the world. That was what was important - not some fleeting desire to kiss a beautiful man...

◆ ◆ ◆

"Do you like to ride, sir?" I asked Lord Lisle as the horses were saddled. I kept my eyes from straying towards the stables, afraid I would see Avery and lose all ability to think straight.

"It's not something I find much time to do," he said, tapping his foot impatiently as he waited for one of our horses to be brought to him. I sighed inwardly as Michael, one of the boys who worked in the stables, brought me Snowflake, ready to ride with a side saddle. Of course, I had known that I would have to use it, but it stopped me being able to ride as fast as I would have liked - although, considering my fall the previous day, perhaps that wasn't such a bad thing.

Once Michael had brought Mischief, a horse that was far more gentle that his name suggested, for Lord Lisle, he offered me help onto my horse - but Lord Lisle shooed him away, and my heart sank as I realised he meant to help me himself. It reminded me too much of the feeling of Avery helping me back onto Snowflake - and somehow I did not think Lord Lisle would engender the same feelings.

The little wooden step stool was already out, and although I could have hoisted myself on without any help, it certainly would not have been dignified. As Lord Lisle offered me his arm, I saw father smiling atop his mount, and reminded myself that I needed to make this work.

"Thank you," I said with a smile, taking hold of his hand and positioning myself in the side saddle, with my dress draped over my legs.

"My pleasure," he said, and I tried not to watch as he attempted to mount his horse three times, before accepting help from Michael. When he said he did not ride much, he obviously meant it - but perhaps that was something I could encourage, if we were married. Riding out with a husband seemed like an enjoyable way to spend time - and perhaps he would be keen to do so, since I enjoyed riding so much.

We set off as a group, gently walking the horses through the damp grass and into the trees. There were ten of us in total, with father at the helm, although only three women had chosen to take part. Grace, keen not to be left behind, trotted along with the yeoman's wife, and I was afforded more time with Lord Lisle than I would have chosen myself.

"What a glorious day," he said, as the sun filtered through the trees.

"Indeed," I agreed, trying to think what we could talk about, since horses clearly did not greatly interest him.

"Your mother is not here?" It was a question, although the answer was obvious; I shook my head.

"My lady mother is not so enamoured with riding," I said with a smile. That was something of an understatement; she referred to horses as 'unpredictable beasts', and never rode unless it was completely unavoidable.

"Well, that seems very appropriate for a lady of her standing."

I did not comment, but my visions of riding regularly with my husband were disappearing fast.

In front of me, the slightly doddery-looking Viscount was riding an impressive looking mount - the one, I knew, that Avery had been tasked with taking care of. I did not blame the Viscount for wanting to take such good care of the horse, for he was clearly an experienced mount and even as we gently picked our way through the leaves, showed a refined air that was a cut above the rest of the horses. I wondered what he felt like at speed, or jumping over a fallen tree - and it was only when Lord Lisle responded that I realised I had spoken aloud.

"Over a tree? Sounds rather dangerous."

"Mmhmm," I said, gritting my teeth and avoiding any response that would seem out of place.

"I attended a hunt last month," he said. "Kindly hosted by Lord Salisbury. And would you believe it, two women there rode astride! It was quite the talk of the party - although not in a positive light, I can assure you."

"It does seem like it would be easier, to ride like a man, no?" I ventured, but the look on his face suggested my words were not welcome.

"It's not about what is easy, Mistress Isabel, but what is right, don't you think?"

"I-I suppose so."

He smiled then, and I hoped my misstep would be forgotten.

The riders ahead were clearly keen to increase the pace, and father, the Viscount and the yeoman farmer set off at a canter, into the woodland that stretched for miles. Not all of it belonged to us, but it was all used for leisurely pursuits by those who lived near, and it was so large we seldom ran into anyone else.

Normally I would have joined them, but Lord Lisle seemed happy to keep to a walk and so, along with my sister and the yeoman's wife, we meandered through the trees, before coming to a stream that the horses were keen to drink from.

In the distance I could hear laughter and the heavy thud of hooves, and beneath me I felt Snowflake, eager to stretch her legs and join the band of horses ahead.

Alas, we were both to be disappointed.

"Shall we turn back?" Lord Lisle suggested after half an hour or so. "I would love to take a stroll around the gardens with you - on foot," he said with a smile. "There is something I wish to discuss."

We left Grace, who was happily in discussion about the latest court fashions, which she had heard about from a friend who had recently gone to serve Queen Anne, and turned the horses for home. I resisted the urge to push Snowflake into a trot, and internally promised both her and myself that we would find some time for a decent ride soon.

One where I would not fall off.

The stables were quiet, with every horse in use, and Lord Lisle half-fell from his horse before offering to help me down. I wondered if this was to be my life; accepting help for things I could do perfectly well myself because of propriety.

His arm went around my waist, and I shivered with a revulsion I tried desperately to suppress.

"Oi, you there," he shouted, and I cringed at the tone of his voice. "Can you not see these horses need to be seen to?"

We had barely touched the ground, and I turned, hoping I could apologise to poor Michael without being seen - but was even more horrified when I realised it was Avery he was speaking to.

Avery who did not even work for us.

Avery who was looking at him with such a look of contempt, I was afraid Lord Lisle would have him struck off.

"Shall we walk?" I said quickly, keen to separate the two, and with a parting pat on the nose for

Snowflake, I took his offered arm and walked the short distance to the gardens.

The flowerbeds were mother's pride and joy; she'd cultivated them herself over the year we had been here, and even when she let the gardener do his work, she always kept a close eye on their progress. Next year she planned a herb garden, and I felt a sadness that I would not be here to see it.

Not if I were Lady Lisle, and ensconced in a manor many, many miles from here.

Across the yard I saw James, the gardener, busy weeding, and the yeoman's daughter - Elizabeth, I remembered her name was - taking a walk, but the majority of the party were still out riding, and I knew Mother would be busy making sure everything was ready for another feast tonight. Everything had to reflect our new status as people of wealth - and Mother had never let Father down when it came to being a good hostess.

"I think you know what I wish to talk to you about," he said, stopping beneath the arched window of the house. "And although I must speak formally with your father, it would be my honour if you would be betrothed to be my wife. I wanted to see you, and spend time with you, before agreeing to this match, but I believe we will suit well together, and that you will be a fine mother to my sons, as well as filling the nursery with many more Lisles."

I had not expected to be faced with this so soon, so bluntly, but I knew what my answer must be. My father would arrange all the details, of course, and I tried to not think about whether I would even have been considered by Lord Lisle if it had not been for my generous dowry. I looked to the floor, the picture of modesty, and felt my cheeks blush red.

"I would be honoured, my lord," I said, and he hooked a finger under my chin so I would raise my head and look at him.

He smiled, and I hoped there was kindness underneath everything else. I supposed I could cope with everything else, as long as he was kind - although I had not seen much evidence of it yet. I would just have to hope.

He moved towards me, and I knew what he planned, although the air did not crackle with promise as it had done when Avery had kissed me in the great hall, or when he we had been so close to kissing in the stables on Christmas Day.

I closed my eyes, and hoped he would take my reticence for innocence. His lips pressed against mine, hot and wet and I stood there, thanking the lord that we were in the open and he would surely not want to impugn my honour or be seen to be taking advantage.

A voice in the back of my head reminded me that, once we were married, he could do whatever he pleased.

And that thought made me shudder.

He pulled away, a smile on his lips that did not make me feel any better, and placed my hand back on his arm as he walked us in the direction of the front door.

"I will speak to your father this evening. We will be betrothed on Twelfth Night, and married soon after - I will arrange everything. I am keen for you to meet my sons - they have sorely missed having a mother."

My heartstrings were pulled at that; perhaps being a mother was something I could throw myself into. As hazy as I was on the details, the physical side of marriage was something that sent a shudder of fear through me - but perhaps motherhood, and step-motherhood, could be a silver lining.

If I was going to be married to this man, I felt I was going to need to look out for the silver linings.

❖ ❖ ❖

Mother came to me as I was preparing for the ball, clad in a beautiful red dress and hood that made her look more youthful than her years, as

Hettie was finishing brushing out my long, blonde hair.

I smiled, and as Mother politely dismissed Hettie, I realised with a start that mother was younger than my prospective husband. What a thought…

"You look lovely, Mother," I said, and turned to face her as she sat down on the edge of my bed.

"Thank you, dear. You look wonderful in that dress - is Hettie going to do something with your hair?"

"Some braids, I think."

"Lovely. Now, I am sure you're not surprised, but Lord Lisle has approached your father."

My breath caught in my throat, and mother reached across to take my hand.

"This is wonderful news, Isabel. You will be a lady, in charge of your own manor, and your children will have such opportunities. And think of the match your sister can make, especially if we are invited to court."

I nodded, not wanting to say the words that were in my head, but knowing if I didn't, I might always regret it.

"He's so much older than me…"

She nodded, and there was sympathy in her

eyes. "I know. But age isn't everything. You must look to his personality, and to finding what you may have in common. This is a great honour - and we are all so proud of you."

"Thank you," I said, knowing there was nothing more for me to say.

"Now," she said. "You will have a wonderful time this evening, and I'm sure you will dazzle Lord Lisle in that dress."

As she left the room, Hettie reappeared, and as she deftly pinned the front of my hair in intricate braids, I examined my reflection. The dress was stunning - further proof of the money my father had, and how he was willing to spend it to see a daughter well-married - in a beautiful deep blue, with intricate beading around the square neckline and flashes of paler blue through the skirt. It was designed to attract attention, and although it seemed the deal was already done, I supposed it couldn't hurt to look my very best.

It was to be my last Christmas as an unwed lady, and I was determined to enjoy it.

CHAPTER FOURTEEN

Avery

It was a far bigger event than any I'd been to; as a boy, I had been very much on the outside of warm, inviting homes at Christmas, sneaking a peek in if I were lucky. And since I'd been with the Viscount, he had done little entertaining - and so I had not been expected to attend any such event. However, I had made my way in this world by learning how to fit in, and so I followed the lead of the other servants, who entered the great hall in a jubilant fashion. We were wearing our best clothes, although they were nothing compared to the gentry around us, and there was a thrill in the air at the barriers between us and them being lowered a little, albeit temporarily.

The room was decorated as it had been when I had helped to bring in the Yule Log, which was happily burning away in the grate, and I smiled at the sight of that kissing bough which had filled my dreams.

A feast was set out across several tables, and candles were lit to let everyone enjoy the evening despite the early darkness of the season.

I stayed with the group, who were awaiting the master of the house to enter. I saw the Viscount and nodded politely, and was surprised to see him making his way towards me.

"Merry Christmas, Avery," he said, and I bent my head.

"Thank you, my lord. Merry Christmas to you."

"Shadow road well today. Has he been in good form?"

"Very good, my lord - and I am pleased to hear that. He's a fine horse."

"He is indeed." And with that he moved on, but I felt a sense of pride that it was me he wanted to talk about Shadow with. Near the fireplace, I spotted Lord Lisle, who had already shouted at me twice today. Not a pleasant man, I suspected - and not a man who knew anything about horses.

Not a man who should be marrying a woman like Isabel...

Everyone turned as the Radcliffes entered; Mr and Mrs Radcliffe first, arm in arm, followed by their daughters. Isabel was resplendent in a blue dress, and my eyes could not be torn away from her. She was a rare jewel, and I knew that she would be married soon, even if the proposed betrothal to Lord Lisle did not go ahead. She was beautiful, she was young, and rumour had it she had a very generous dowry. There were enough men of the gentry who would have been happy with the first two, but the third would surely seal the deal. No-one would care that she had a merchant's background, and she would propel her family further into the higher levels of society.

The light from the candles made her hair seem to glow golden, and the smile on her face warmed my heart in a way I had never really known before. It was dangerous, to think about a woman this much - and yet I could not help myself.

The buzz in the room faded as it became clear Mr Radcliffe wished to speak. "My lords, ladies, family and friends. It is our great honour to spend the Christmas season with you all, and to host this feast for you all."

There was a round of applause, and both Mr and Mrs Radcliffe beamed at the crowd of guests. "We thought we might prevail upon a tradition from court this evening," Mr Radcliffe continued. "To make sure we have the merriest of times. A Lord of Misrule!"

A whisper went through the crowd: we had all heard of the custom, even though we had not all been part of a household that followed the tradition.

"We shall pick a young man to lead the festivities, and his word tonight shall be law!"

He gazed around the audience, and I wondered if he had already picked the unlucky man who would be on display for all to see. But from the look on his face he was choosing now and, knowing that a Lord of Misrule was traditionally not from the higher classes, I took a step to the side, hoping to be out of his eye-line.

"Do we have any suggestions for who will make an excellent Lord of Misrule?" the lady of the house was asking, and I was astonished to hear the Viscount shouting out a name - my name.

"Avery. Over there."

He pointed in my direction, and I felt my cheeks redden. I had no experience of court, and the Viscount had never held Christmas in great style - I had only gossip to guide me.

"He looks like an excellent choice," Mr Radcliffe was saying, and I caught Isabel's eye, feeling a little gratified that her cheeks turned a beautiful pink as her eyes met mine.

"I- I'm not sure I'm the best-" But it was no use. I was surrounded by people I did not know, who wrapped a thick fur cloak around my shoulders and shoved a crown of evergreens onto my head, and suddenly I was the centre of attention.

I could feel Isabel's eyes on me, but I did not look at her; I could not be distracted by her now, when the eyes of everyone were upon me.

"What shall be your first declaration, my lord?" It was Isabel's sister who asked, and I racked my brains for something simple that could give me time to think how to best use this weighty title.

"A dance!" I said finally. "Everyone must join in!"

There was little grumbling on this merry night, as the musicians struck up a lively number that I thankfully recognised. A simple country dance, but hopefully one the majority would know. Even I had danced it before, although it had not been for a long while.

My eyes alighted on Isabel, but my heart sank as she was immediately partnered by Lord Lisle. I should have known...

But then, I thought, as I paired with a fine looking lady I believed was a daughter of one the guests, I was a lord for tonight. The Lord of Misrule. And I planned to turn that to my advantage...

CHAPTER FIFTEEN
Isabel

I tried to focus on what Lord Lisle was saying, but in truth I was finding it hard to keep my gaze away from Avery. He looked as handsome as ever, clad in a fine cloak and ivy crown, and watching him dance - or trying not to watch, as the case may be - I could see a fun-loving side to him that had been hidden to me.

"Still no son," Lord Lisle was saying in hushed tones as we performed the steps. Thankfully, I'd practised with my dance master so many times that I could have danced it in my sleep - saving my focus for other matters.

"Oh?"

"It's all the talk at court. They say - well, that's probably not for a lady's ears. But the King is well within his rights, of course, as any man is, to investigate the validity of his marriage. He is worried, I believe, in case there is a reason why they have not been blessed with a son."

My attention was caught, although he spoke of matters I had only heard mentioned in passing.

"A son? But how will questioning his marriage solve that?"

He looked at me as if I were addled, and I felt annoyance prickle through me.

"Why, because if this second marriage were not valid, he would be free to remarry."

"Remarry?"

"Hush!" he said, glancing around to make sure no-one had heard. "I am trusting you, as the woman I shall become betrothed to. I would not have spoken so freely with anyone else."

"I thank you for your trust," I said, not sad that the dance required a switch of partners. Round and round I danced, joining in the circles before being faced with my partner for the next dance.

The Lord of Misrule himself.

CHAPTER SIXTEEN

Avery

It was as if fate had stepped in to ensure we would meet, and as our hands touched I felt a desire that shocked me with its intensity. Here in this great hall, with the distinction of class temporarily dissolved by the festive season, I felt bold. Yes, she would be marrying someone else - but I decided to enjoy the time I could spend around her, while I could. It would give me some good memories to think back on as I worked hard to improve my lot in the coming years.

"Good evening, my lady," I said, bowing my head and enjoying the blush that spread across her cheeks and décolletage.

"Good evening, my lord," she said, and although the words were only true for tonight, they sounded wonderful in her soft voice.

"You look beautiful," I said, meaning every word, and she smiled as our hands touched once more.

"You look very dashing, as the Lord of Misrule."

"I would not have chosen the title myself… but it has some advantages."

"Oh?" Her eyes widened and a slow grin spread across my face. "Like what?"

"You'll see," I said.

And then she was gone, to flit among another group until she landed on her next partner, and I was left to contemplate my little slice of power this evening.

CHAPTER SEVENTEEN
Isabel

As the night continued, my anticipation grew. He looked happy, and relaxed, and managed to be far more collected in front of me than I was in front of him.

I knew I needed to put him from my mind, but tonight he was everywhere, and that would not be possible. No, I gave myself tonight to be entranced by him. He was the Lord of Misrule, everyone was paying him court and fawning over him. My eyes would not be noticed amongst so many.

I would give myself tonight, and tomorrow I would move on.

He stepped into the role with surprising ease, although I was sure he was pleased father had not crowned him for the whole twelve nights, nor made him responsible for all the festive revelry. No, he had tonight, and he seemed to easily involve everyone despite the range of ages and levels of status in the room.

He had us exchange an item of clothing, which resulted in much giggling and me wearing my mother's hood for a time. There was another dance, although he did not take part, and then he commanded everyone to feast, drink and be merry, and for a while everyone's attention moved to the food and the plentiful wine.

My eyes did not leave him, and once I noticed Lord Lisle busily ensconced in a conversation with my father - although the content of such a conversation made me a little nervous - I took my wine and comfits and made my way to stand beside him.

"You are doing an excellent job," I told him. "I've not seen all the guests this happy since they arrived!"

He smiled; "It's not my usual area of skill, but I'm trying."

"All the power… it must be thrilling."

"Do you not have power?"

I sighed; "As a woman? Not really."

He nodded and was silent for a moment.

"Tell me a secret," he said, his voice as rich and warm as the chestnuts toasted in the fireplace.

"Pardon?"

"As the Lord of Misrule... I command it." He smiled, and I felt my heart soar.

"Well. As Lord of Misrule..." I thought for a moment, and then let slip the only secret I really had - but one which most definitely should not have been passing my lips.

"I wish..." I said, in a whisper so low he had to lean in to hear it. "I wish I did not have to marry Lord Lisle."

The words had a sobering affect, and we were both quiet for a spell, watching the rest of the room make merry while the truth I had spoken hung in the air.

He checked to make sure no-one was watching, then let his hand brush against mine for just a moment.

The illicit contact sent warmth through my body and I felt an ache when he pulled back.

"You tell me one," I finally said.

"That is not really in keeping with the tradition."

"Please?" My eyes met his, and I knew I had won.

"Fine. I lived on the streets as a child - until I was eleven."

The shock showed on my face, I was sure, and I

became less aware of the guests around us.

"On the streets? What about your parents?"

"They died of the plague when I was little. My brother and I - we fended for ourselves, but he also succumbed."

"Where?"

"London - easiest place to steal food."

The thought of Avery as a little boy, with no home and no parents, nearly broke my heart. "I'm so sorry."

"Does it make me too low for you to talk to?"

"Avery..." I said. "I would never think that. I am just sorry you had such a tough childhood."

"Well. I've improved things, since then..." he said. "And I plan to improve my lot further - who knows, maybe one day you and Lord Lisle will be inviting me round as a guest!"

I tried to smile, but the thought was not a happy one. Not the idea of him being our guest, but the idea of being Lady Lisle.

CHAPTER EIGHTEEN

Avery

Hearing her say those words had been harder than I'd expected. I'd suspected, of course, that she would not choose Lord Lisle if it were her decision, but to hear that she was going into a marriage so completely against her wishes...

I watched Lord Lisle for a moment, as he spoke with the Viscount. He was not the sort of man I imagined the Viscount would have much patience with, and I was pleased when I saw him turned away fairly quickly.

Then he turned to approach us, and I had another idea.

I took three steps into the centre of the room, and shouted. "Another dance!" The musicians looked at me, waiting for me to declare the type of music needed.

"The volt!" someone shouted in the back of the room, and there was a gasp; even I had heard of the volt, a dance that required couples to embrace, as the gentleman lifted the lady through the air. But I did not know the volt...

"If someone can demonstrate, I am sure the rest of us can follow," I said, knowing what my next declaration would be. Lively music began, and the volunteers - a couple I did not know, but who were definitely not from the servants hall, began to move elegantly through the space, and then his hands were on her waist and he was lifting her round, as though she were air.

A few moments more, and everyone was keen to participate, and as Lord of Misrule I turned to Isabel.

"I shall dance with the most beautiful lady in the room," I said, sweeping her a bow and offering my hand. She smiled, and took my hand, and in that moment the world felt right. This act of courtly love was applauded by all as they took their partners, and for this one night we could behave in ways that would not be acceptable in the cold light of day. Tonight, no-one thought of us as anything more than two revellers.

Our eyes were locked, and as the music began we stepped together, forwards and back, around the other couples, and I wondered if she had already learnt this dance in her lessons. It was new to me, of course, but repetitive, and I prided myself on learning quickly. It had got me this far, and as my hand encircled her waist and lifted her into the air, I knew my stint as Lord of Misrule would stay in my mind for a long time to come.

I lowered her, our lips so close, but then we stepped again and the room came back into my awareness. We were not perhaps as invincible as I felt; I was sure Lord Lisle was glaring at me at every chance he got.

"I love Christmas," she said with a smile, speaking quietly so that only I could hear.

"Before this year, I'd not felt strongly about it. But now…"

She blushed, and for a moment I wondered what would happen if I threw caution to the wind and kissed her, right here, in front of so many people.

Would they laugh off such a shocking act from their own-crowned Lord?

I doubted it.

When I next lifted her, her lips were at my ear, and I felt a shiver flutter through me, both at her proximity and the words she whispered.

"Meet me in the gardens. After this dance."

I nodded, the only sign I gave that I had heard her words, but my focus on the dance was all but ruined.

CHAPTER NINETEEN
Isabel

I shivered, both from the cold air and the anticipation at seeing him here, in the moonlit garden, away from so many eyes. I had given myself this night, and the words had not been planned, but I could not be sorry they had slipped from my mouth.

He was so beautiful. It was not a word I had used about a man before, but he was: his ebony black hair, the strong muscles in his arms, his perfect jawline...

But he was also kind. He had helped me, he had kept my secret, he had made me feel like I could open up to him about anything...

What was this secret assignation? Even I was not sure. But as I saw him hurrying out towards me moments after I had left the hall, I could not question myself.

"Isabel..." he murmured as he reached me. The moonlight gave away my location, and I took his hand and pulled him around the house, where shadows reigned and I could be sure no-one could see us.

Even this would ruin me - but I could not enter marriage to a man I did not love, did not desire, without knowing the true kiss of Avery. I knew that now, and it was all I could think of, even if I could not imagine how to put it into words.

"Avery..." I said, taking a step towards him.

"You must be freezing," he said, noticing I had no cloak, and before I could reply his cloak of Misrule was around my shoulders, and I felt his warmth and his scent enveloping me.

"I have never enjoyed a night like I have tonight," he said, reaching a hand up to touch the braid that sat so close to my ear. I closed my eyes, feeling the warmth of his fingers as our breath swirled mistily in front of us.

Boldly, I removed my glove, and pressed my hand to his chest. The lawn shirt felt rough beneath my hand, but I could feel his heat, even through the fabric.

"Avery... I must marry him."

"I know."

"But I feel…"

He took a step forward and smiled, although there was a hint of sadness to his eyes that I could not ignore. "I know."

And then I could no longer speak. His fingers moved to the back of my neck, entwining with my hair, and his lips pressed to mine.

My hand was still upon his chest, and to begin with it felt like that kiss in the great hall, although with no audience this time. And then I let my arms move around his neck, pulling him closer, and as his tongue touched to mine I felt as though my legs might melt beneath me.

Desire built inside me, hot, white and so new. My hands found that ebony hair and as my lips moved with his, my body pressed closer, needing him like I needed the air to breathe.

Somehow I moved to lean against the wall, and I appreciated its cold strength that stopped me sliding to the floor. As we both needed to draw breath, his lips moved to my neck, and the stars above me were nothing to those that were whizzing around in my head, making me positively dizzy.

"Avery," I said, not sure what else to say but only knowing I had never in my life felt like this.

He stopped, then, and I regretted speaking, because nothing had ever felt so heavenly as the feel of his lips on mine, his hands around my waist, his solid body pressed against me in a way that felt deliciously wrong...

Our eyes met, only the light of the moon illuminating his face, and at the smile on his lips, I could not help but smile too.

"Isabel..." he said, stroking the back of his hand down the side of my face, and I leaned in to his embrace, soaking up every second of his warmth before this magical night was over.

"One more kiss," I said, smiling at my own boldness. "And then you, my lord, will have to return to your people."

"If I could have one wish," he said, his hands resting on my waist like they were made to fit there, pulling me closer still; "It would be for this moment to last forever."

I felt as though I couldn't breathe, and then his lips were upon mine again, and all rational thought was gone.

It was only for tonight - but oh, what a night it had been.

CHAPTER TWENTY

Avery

I awoke the next morning from the most peaceful sleep I could remember having in a long time, and it took me a while to fathom why I felt so contented.

Memories of my evening flooded back, and I could have been a king on a feather mattress for how light I felt. Yes, it was but for one night, but the feel of her skin, her lips beneath mine, her body pressed against me...

For a man who had spent his life honing self-preservation instincts, I had certainly slipped up this time. If we had been caught together, pressed up against the solid stone walls, she would have been ruined - and I fired, I was sure. And yet there was something about her, something I did not truly understand, that made me throw caution to the wind.

It had only been for the night, I knew that - but

I could not help but let my imagination run wild, after realising that all the desire I had felt for her was returned.

CHAPTER TWENTY-ONE

Isabel

"Good morning, Mistress Isabel."

As I made my way down the steps, a little later than usual thanks to the late hour at which I had gone to bed, I was dismayed to see Lord Lisle waiting at the bottom of the staircase. I had managed to evade him last night, after my assignation with Avery, and seeing him now I knew I should feel guilt, or remorse, but I was ashamed to say I felt neither.

No, all I felt was a crushing sense of disappointment that the night I had allowed myself was over, and I must return to the harsh reality before me.

I smiled, hoping it seemed genuine.

"Good morning, Lord Lisle."

"I think you should probably call me Francis, if we're to be betrothed, my dear."

I nodded, but could not quite let the name pass through my lips.

"Would you accompany me around the gardens, once you have broken your fast?" he asked me, falling into step beside me as I walked towards the great hall.

"I'm afraid I must decline, my lord," I said. "I traditionally always deliver alms to the poor - and I have arranged to go today. Of course, you are more than welcome to join me."

I wondered how bad it was that I was praying for him to say no.

He grimaced, and stopped short of the table. "I think not," he said.

I should have left it, and considered my prayer answered, for it would have made things so much simpler.

But of course, I could not.

"May I ask why?" I asked, as breakfast was brought to me by a young boy. I nodded my head in thanks.

"Not to take away from your endeavours, my lady," he said, giving me a courtesy title that, as yet, did not belong to me. "But with the uprisings against the King recently... I am not sure the poor deserve your charity."

"But surely," I said, "Christmas is a time of forgiveness, and generosity? I could not bear to think of a family with nothing to eat while we feast."

He smiled a threadbare grin, that stretched across his face and almost looked painful to hold there. "And I commend you for your charity. We must consider, however, whether people are truly deserving, and whether they in fact deserve the place they have been given in God's land."

I stared at my plate, mulling over his words. Surely he did not mean them as they sounded? That the poor deserved to be poor - and should be left to remain so?

I opened my mouth once more, saw the look on his face and promptly closed it. He had already made it clear he did not approve of women adventuring, or taking part in politics - and I was sure no further comment on my part would be taken well.

"I shall see you later, then, my lord," I said, not able to say his first name without shuddering at the implied intimacy. Approve of my activities he might not - but I was not under his orders.

Not yet.

◆ ◆ ◆

I looked for him when I went to the stables, but

he was nowhere to be seen. It was probably for the best; I did not know what good could possibly come from me seeing him this morning, but after Lord Lisle's harsh words, I felt I wanted to see a friendly face.

Instead, a young lad saddled up Snowflake for me, along with Grace's horse (a grey mare she had named 'Mouse' several years ago), and by the time they were ready, Grace had appeared along with another lad who was carrying the baskets of food and clothes that we traditionally took to the poor over the festive period. Even when we had lived in a much smaller abode, father had always extolled the virtues of giving to those less fortunate, and it was something I tried to do monthly - but at this time of year it was always welcomed the most. When the world was so cold, the crops so bare and festive cheer was needed, our charity brought even more smiles.

"Ready?" I asked Grace, and we both mounted side-saddle, although with Grace in tow I knew we would not be travelling fast however we were saddled. She did not dislike riding, but was quite happy to take it slowly, taking in the surroundings and getting inspiration for her latest painting. Whereas I loved the thrill of riding hard and fast, jumping lakes, trees, once even a bridge...

She smiled, wearing a simple day dress and a heavy cloak to protect her against the chill.

"Ready!" she said with a grin, and together we turned the horses towards the local village, baskets balanced in front of us - another reason for a slow journey.

In the distance, my eye was caught by a black shape moving through the trees, and a grin spread across my face as I wondered if it were Avery, riding the magnificent Shadow. I guessed the old Viscount would not have been up for regularly exercising him, and a mount like that would need regular exercise…

"Did you find out his name, in the end?" Grace was asking, and my eyes were torn from the horizon as I turned to face her.

"Who?"

She rolled her eyes and grinned. "The man you kissed under the kissing bough!" she exclaimed, and I felt the heat rushing to my cheeks.

"Grace, shush!"

"Why? Is it a secret?"

I sighed; of course, there hadn't technically been anything wrong with that kiss… but the ones that had followed, the ones that had heated my blood and invaded my dreams - they would certainly not be approved of.

"It's just… you know I am to be betrothed. Well,

Lord Lisle might not like it."

"You're not married yet," she said, and I tried not to let her know how close to my own thoughts that was.

"Well, I would not wish to upset him," I said primly, hoping I was setting a good example for my wayward little sister. After all, this marriage would bring about great things for her - although I did not want to burden her with those thoughts over Christmas.

"I saw you talking, at the ball - wasn't he a brilliant Lord of Misrule! So I just wondered if you found out his name."

I weighed my options, but in the end saw no reason she should not know his name. It would look odd if we'd spent the night conversing - and dancing - without exchanging names.

"Avery," I said, liking the sound of it on my lips.

"Avery," my sister replied, then sighed. "He is very handsome…"

"And I'm sure it is not appropriate for you to be commenting on such a thing!" I said, blushing a little. He was more handsome that I knew how to handle… I had seen the other ladies, both high and low born, eying him last night. Inexperienced or not, I recognised a good-looking man when I saw one. But that was a dangerous path to let my mind traverse.

"Let's focus on doing some good in our community," I said. "I believe Mrs Laith lost her husband earlier this year, so they may be struggling - let's start there, see if the children need any of these clothes."

CHAPTER TWENTY-TWO
Avery

Both Shadow and I returned covered in a sheen of sweat from our exertions, but my mind felt clearer than it had done in a while. Letting Shadow show off his full potential often did that, I found, and after such a peaceful night's sleep, I had needed to get out and burn some energy. He had approached every jump, every turn, every gallop with the same beautiful grace he always did - and I felt he was as content as I was as I rubbed him down and gave him a carrot I'd nabbed from the kitchens.

I noticed Snowflake was not in her stall, nor a grey mare that was usually next to her, and could not help my mind from wondering where she might be. Hopefully the fact that two horses were absent meant she was not alone, and at risk of a dangerous fall once more - although I hoped heartily it were not Lord Lisle who was accompanying her. I mistrusted the man - and it wasn't just because I wanted to kiss the woman he planned to marry. There was something about him that did not sit well with me...

With manual work banned for the festive period, I had more free time on my hands than I was used to, and apart from another feast with the servants later that day - where some card games had been proposed - I had the rest of the day free. Deciding I would make the most of how warm I was, I took a clean set of clothes and headed to a lake I had found while out riding. It would be bracing indeed, but it was the easiest way to get clean, and I had the warm coat Isabel had brought me for afterwards.

I checked carefully to make sure no-one was around once I had made my way - on foot this time - to the little lake, and stripped down to my under garments. It certainly would not do to be discovered in the nude! I took a deep breath and stepped into the cold water. Its iciness ensured I did not linger, but the plunge beneath the surface of the water washed away the sweat and grime and made me feel altogether refreshed.

Water dripping from my hair, I exited swiftly and quickly divested myself of the wet garments, replacing them with clean, dry clothes and that thick coat Isabel had brought me. The warmth it gave was from more than just the fur - knowing she had cared enough to bring me clothes made my heart feel full.

CHAPTER TWENTY-THREE

Isabel

As we approached the stables, our journey much easier on the way back thanks to the now empty baskets we carried, I turned to Grace.

"Why don't you go in and change for dinner," I suggested. "I can make sure the horses are settled."

She didn't question whether there was an ulterior motive, and for that I was grateful. She dismounted and skipped off towards the house, and I watched her for a moment, wishing I could be as carefree as she was.

I slid off Snowflake, and led the two horses by their reins, my heart fluttering. Would he be here now? I felt a need to see him that I could not explain, and although I did not know what I would say if I saw him, I hoped beyond reason that he would be in the stables.

"Avery?" I whispered, when it seemed the stable was empty, save for the horses - but there was no response.

My mood dropped, and with dread in my heart at the thought of dinner that evening next to Lord Lisle, I began to put the two horses away, wondering where the young lad who normally tended to our horses was. I didn't begrudge him the time off, and I sincerely hoped the time alone would help me to get in a better frame of mind for the evening's festivities. Tonight would be a quieter night, although there might well be singing and dancing - but the big New Year's feast, with the requisite exchanging of gifts, was what everyone was looking forward to now; that, and the Twelfth Night revels, when I knew father had booked mummers to perform a play for us all.

Somehow, I could not summon the excitement I had a week ago. How had everything changed since Christmas Eve?

"Isabel." The sound of my name on his lips made me whirl around, startling Snowflake until I put my hand to her warm flank to calm her.

I smiled; I couldn't help it.

"Avery."

We both stepped at the same time, neither voicing all the issues with this meeting, both caught up in a moment that was so much bigger than either of us.

"You weren't here this morning, when I left," I said.

"I was exercising Shadow," he said, and I noticed his hair was damp. I wondered if he'd fallen, but the rest of him showed no sign of a fall. I wished I could see him ride; I could imagine it was an impressive sight.

I smiled, and without thinking reached up to touch his ebony hair. How it had become an instinct to do something like that - something I never would have done before this week - I did not know, but I wanted to feel it between my fingertips.

It was damp, as I had suspected, and his eyes closed as my fingers combed through it, before landing on the hollow of his throat.

He swallowed, and I blushed at my boldness. "I'm sorry," I said - but I did not remove my hand. "I don't know what's got into me."

"You don't need to apologise," he said, taking a step closer. His breath hitched as I let my fingers trail to where his lawn shirt opened at the neck, and I felt my pulse race. I had no idea what I was doing, but oh god did it feel good. This handsome man stood in front of me, not questioning my brazen touch, not saying a word, just letting me do what I needed...

And I needed him. I did not know why, but I did - and staying away had not worked so far.

"Can I kiss you?" he asked, a huskiness in his voice, and I nodded, not trusting myself to speak.

His hands rested on my waist, and for a moment his dark eyes met mine. I felt like he could see everything that was hidden beneath the thin veneer of respectability I had been trying to keep intact - and then his lips touched mine.

He was slow, and sweet, and the heat grew between us even though it was a much calmer kiss than the one that had consumed us the night before. I took a step backwards and found myself leaning against a hay bale, and let his hands and the hay take most of my weight as I gave myself to that kiss. I did not think about everything that was wrong with this moment, but let the feeling of it being oh so right consume me. My hands, without much thought, began to wander the planes of his back, feeling the well-worked muscles through the thin material of his shirt.

Avery lifted me so I was sat on the hay, and although I let out a squeak of surprise, his lips did not leave mine, and I soon forgot the move and just enjoyed how close it allowed us to be. Scandalously, he stepped forwards until he was between my legs, and I felt his fingers touching my ankle with a feather light touch, where the dress had hitched up and bared some skin.

I broke the kiss, unable to focus on so many sensations - his sturdy body stood so close to me, his lips on mine, his fingers on my ankle, and he paused for a second. I smiled, then let my head loll backwards as he pressed his lips to my throat.

I groaned. This felt too good. Was this what marriage entailed? If things could feel this amazing, it was a wonder anyone left the bedchamber.

Unbidden, the image of Lord Lisle entered my head, and I pushed it away. Somehow, I did not think marriage would be anything like this.

His fingers fluttered up the back of my leg, and there was something so intimate in a man touching somewhere that was always covered by skirts and kirtles and that no-one had ever paid much attention to, that I gasped.

He dropped his hand, obviously taking it as a bad sign, and although I longed for him to continue, I had a feeling we were heading towards a point of no return - a point I could not afford to cross.

No matter how much I might want to.

CHAPTER TWENTY-FOUR

Avery

I could not believe what had happened, and her gasp made me realise suddenly what a compromising position we were in…

And how close I had come to compromising her honour.

There was something about her that just made me lose my mind, and as I took a step away, my breath coming out in jagged bursts, I was pleased to see her smile - even if it were accompanied with a blush.

She stepped off the hay, readjusted her dress, and I reached forward and plucked a piece of straw from her hair.

"I'm sorry," I said, putting my hands behind my back to try to resist any further temptations.

"You don't need to be sorry," she said, echoing

my earlier words, and I smiled.

"I should not have gone so far..."

"I wasn't stopping you," she said, and in that moment I saw a strong, independent young woman - even if society was trying to stop her being so.

"Shall we talk?" I suggested, and she nodded, sitting herself back onto the hay bale and tapping it for me to join her. Instead, I pulled an empty crate over and perched on it; I did not trust myself in such close proximity.

"Where did you go today?" I asked, trying to get my mind back onto more mundane topics, and get my mind off the thought of taking her up to the pallet I slept on...

No. It would not do to let my mind wander there. She was not some maid who knew exactly what she was getting into; this was a respectable woman who was to marry a lord - and I needed to remember that. For both of our sakes.

◆ ◆ ◆

"I was delivering food and clothes to some of the less fortunate residents of the local village," I said. "It's something Grace and I have done every year..."

He smiled at that, and I was pleased he did not

echo any of the sentiments Lord Lisle had shared earlier.

"A worthy cause," he said. "As someone who has been in some very unfortunate circumstances over the festive period, I would have been very grateful for someone like you."

I reached out and took his hand, unable to help myself at the thought of him on the streets as a young boy.

"It's a terrible thing," I whispered, "That some should have so much, and some so little."

He nodded, turning my hand over and holding it in his. Mine seemed very small and soft compared to his, and his work out in the sun meant mine was much paler too. I struggled to focus as his thumb brushed across the delicate bare skin, and I remembered we were supposed to be talking.

"Lord Lisle feels the poor should solve their own problems," I said, knowing I should not be bad-mouthing the man to Avery but at the same time not knowing who else I could share these worries with. How could I have begun to trust someone so completely in such a few short days?

Avery made a noise of disgust and paused in his stroking of my palm. "The man is an idiot," he said. "And has obviously never known what it is like to go hungry."

I nodded; he was right. I had also never known what it was like to wonder where my next meal would come from - but I hoped I had more compassion for those who were in dire straits than Lord Lisle.

❖ ❖ ❖

"I can't marry him," she suddenly said, and for the first time there was a sudden spark of hope in the air. She had voiced her distaste in the match but this - this was something else.

A tear rolled down her cheek as her eyes met mine. "How can I marry him? We are so different - in age, in beliefs, in interests. All he wants is my dowry, and to have an heir - and then I'm sure he'll take a mistress while I'm locked away miles from home in some run down country house." She took a deep breath, but I did not interrupt; she needed to say this, and as much as it hurt to hear it, I did not want to stop her. "I mean," she continued, "It's not as if, as a wife, you can do the same, is it? No, and yet when you're the man, all anyone cares about is you getting an heir…"

She blushed then, and put a hand to her mouth. "I'm sorry," she said. "I should not have said that. It was totally inappropriate."

I smiled; "Don't apologise. You're right - the world is unfair in many ways, not just between the rich and the poor."

"You always seem to understand," she said, and then she was crying in earnest, and the most natural thing in the world was to envelop her in my arms and hold her close. She buried her head in my shoulder and I pressed my lips to the top of her head, wondering how on earth I had got myself in this position, where the happiness of Isabel Radcliffe was so important to me.

For several moments I held her, trying to ignore the way I felt when she was so close to me. Instead, I stroked her hair and tried to think of anything that could improve this situation, that could make her happy, that could give her the future she deserved.

"Could you speak to your father? Tell him you can't marry Lord Lisle?"

She shook her head and sniffed. "I don't think so," she whispered. "They're all pinning their hopes for being accepted in higher society on me. Besides, if I'm not married, they can't really marry off Grace, either - so I'm even more of a burden if I'm unmarried."

I took her hand once more. "They're your family. I'm sure they don't think of you as a burden."

"I couldn't do it," she said, shaking her head, her eyes red and swollen from her tears. And still she was the most beautiful woman I had ever seen. "I couldn't refuse to marry him... besides, if he wants to, my father could ignore my wishes anyway. It's not like I have any real say. What am I going to do?"

"We could run away," I said. I did not know where the words came from, but there they were, and I could not take them back now.

I didn't want to take them back.

Her eyes met mine, wide with shock. "What?"

I licked my lips. Fear of rejection burnt through my veins, but I had never felt like this about anyone, and if there was a hope of securing her happiness and my own into the bargain, it seemed worth taking a chance.

I took both her hands in mine, to make the most sincere proposal that had ever crossed my lips.

"I will protect you," I promised. "We could leave from here, in the dead of night, and get married. Then no-one can make you marry anyone, because you will already be married." I took a deep breath. "I don't have much, but I have some money saved, and I am happy to work wherever I can. I can't offer you this-" I gestured towards the fancy house, with all its staff and trinkets. "But if you want to escape - I can offer you that."

She seemed frozen where she was, and I wondered what was going through her mind. The words that had crossed my lips were nonsensical, really; an ill thought-out idea that had sprung to my mind at the sight of her distress, but that was rapidly, and dangerously, becoming a fixed image in my mind.

Living with Isabel in a small cottage. A few plants outside, maybe; something to start building towards the future I had always planned. A baby, perhaps, to complete the image of us by the fire…

My heart felt dangerously exposed as I waited for her response.

CHAPTER TWENTY-FIVE

Isabel

No words of love had been exchanged; how could they be? We had known each other but days, and knew so little about one another...

And yet he was offering me a way out. He was offering me a future that did not make me want to hide away from the world. A future with a man who respected me, who understood me, who made my body crave his touch...

Was it desire that made me consider his crazy proposal? Or just a need to escape from what was awaiting me?

"Could we?" I asked, my voice hoarse, my eyes not wavering from his.

"It's Christmas," he said with a smile. "Time for good cheer - and for being happy. If we wanted to, we could do anything."

"Yes."

"Yes?"

I could not believe the words coming from his lips, but they were there, and when I envisioned a life married to Avery - even though it would be a far simpler life than I was used to - I felt anticipation hum through my veins.

Was it love? I did not know... but it was something more powerful than I had ever experienced.

"Before Twelfth Night," I said. "It will have to be before they can have the betrothal."

He nodded, looking a little stunned, and I decided to be brave. Tentatively, I rested the palm of my hand against his cheek, where I could feel the coarse hair that I presumed he shaved. I moved my head closer, pressing my lips to his to seal this pact we had made, and felt my heart sing with joy.

We could learn whatever we needed to along the way; this feeling was enough to make me excited about our future.

He pulled me roughly against him, but I did not protest; no, I threw my arms around his neck and let the sensation overwhelm my senses. What would his skin feel like, underneath that rough lawn shirt? I guessed I would find out... although not tonight.

Unless…

"Isabel?"

We sprang apart, Avery into the shadows, and I quickly checked to make sure my dress did not show any evidence of our tryst. My cheeks were undoubtedly red, but I hoped the darkness falling around us would stop that being too obvious.

"There you are! You've been ages, mother sent me to check everything was all right."

I stepped out into the light, wanting to avoid any chance of Avery being discovered. "Sorry, Grace. I had to tend to the horses…"

I wasn't sure she believed me, but she linked her arm with mine and seemed happy to head back towards the house, telling me about the sweets that had been made for the evening, and how I must hurry to dress for dinner as everyone was ready to go down.

I barely heard a word. I did not dare to glance back, but felt Avery's eyes on me, the promise of what was to come making me feel dizzy.

I would get through this dinner, and then I would plan.

I tried not to think of what it would do to my family; I was afraid it would change my mind from the course I was set on.

CHAPTER TWENTY-SIX

Avery

For several moments I sat, a little in shock.

Somehow, I had offered to marry this beautiful, vulnerable woman who seemed so far out of my reach - and she had said yes.

A smile played on my lips. This day had certainly not turned out how I had planned - but I could not be disappointed. Yes, I had turned my whole world on its head in a heartbeat - but the future in front of me was an exciting one.

I pictured her with her blonde hair streaming behind her as she'd headed back to the main house, and felt a flutter of anticipation. This looked like it would be the best Christmas I had ever celebrated...

CHAPTER TWENTY-SEVEN

Isabel

My heart was all a flutter as I speedily changed for dinner and dashed down the stairs. Thankfully, no-one commented on my tardiness, nor the redness I was sure had not left my cheeks. I tried to keep the smile off my face at the table, but I was not particularly successful. Grace caught my eye and I blushed, turning away so she could not raise suspicion.

I had agreed to marry a man I had only known for days - but then that was exactly what was expected of me with Lord Lisle. And instead I had accepted the proposal of a man who made my blood sing, who made my breath catch, who made me anticipate our wedding night with excitement…

I did not know how I made it through dinner without blurting out what was on my mind, but I tried to smile at the right moments and pleaded a headache when music and cards were suggested, and slipped from the room without my mother and father managing to speak with me. I did not want to see them, if I were honest with myself; they were the people I would be hurting with my actions, and that was not something I could face right now.

But one look at Lord Lisle, this time seated across the table from me, convinced me I was making the only decision I could. After marriage, as I had always known, I would belong to the man I had married - and I could not be at the mercy of this man.

As my foot reached the bottom step of the staircase, I stopped, hearing laughter and singing from the opposite direction. Curiosity took over and, making sure no-one was watching, I slipped down a side corridor which led to the kitchen. I tried to step quietly, but there was no real chance of anyone hearing me over the sounds of revelry. I paused in the dark corridor, watching the group of men, women and children who worked in the house and grounds. The decorations were by no means as sumptuous as those in the great hall, but evergreens were wound round every available surface, and there was even a kissing bough hung in the centre. Around the wooden table, carols were being sung and in a corner, an enthusiastic game of cards was being played by two couples.

I felt him looking at me before I saw him, and when my eyes picked him out on the edge of a wooden bench, I could not help but smile. There was something about him that made my heart light and hopeful - and my pulse begin to race.

I hadn't planned to see him again that night but as he made his way towards me, I wasn't sorry. I took two steps backwards, so I would be hidden by the darkness in the alcove. It would not do for anyone to know our plans before we had left, before we could be married; the last thing I wanted was to be forced into a marriage against my will because someone had found out I planned to flee.

He found me in that alcove, and despite the noise and crowd of people celebrating so close, when his hands settled on my waist I felt as though we were the only two in the world.

"Looks like fun," I said in a low voice, my lips so close to his I could practically taste them.

He smiled, and I could not tear my gaze from them, remembering how they felt on my lips, on my neck, how they might feel on every bare piece of skin they could reach... "It's all right," he said with a shrug. "I had more fun earlier." My cheeks turned even redder, if it were possible, and I struggled to meet his gaze. How could he make me feel so nervous, so excited, so electric in my own skin?

"How was dinner?" he asked.

"I struggled to focus, if I'm honest," I said, and his smile broadened.

"I can't wait to leave with you," he whispered in my ear, and I felt my insides dissolve. I tried to remind myself that there were people just down the corridor, people who would be horrified to find me in this position with Avery…

Emboldened by his words, I raised my hand to his ebony locks and ran my fingers through it, watching as his eyes fluttered closed at my touch. It was a heady power, and I trailed them across his cheekbone, to those lips, stop beneath his earlobe. I had never touched anyone like this, and it made me forget about everything.

Then there were footsteps, and as someone almost reached the alcove, he pressed his lips to mine and my body backwards against the stone, and even before I realised he was effectively hiding me with his own body, my lips were responding and my body was melting into his.

How had I thought this passion could be ignored? I was in danger of giving him everything before our wedding vows had been said - although, if we were betrothed, would it matter? I blushed at my own thoughts, and wondered - not for the first time - at the changes I had gone through since Christmastime had begun.

The footsteps disappeared, and he pulled away,

and although I ached to beg him to continue, I knew I must wait.

"That was close," he said, but his lips still smiled and my heart still melted.

"I should go," I said, when I had regained some control over my senses. "We will leave after the New Year's celebrations - yes?" What if he changed his mind? Not only would I be forced into a life with Lord Lisle, I was also very aware of how quickly my feelings were changing. How much it would hurt to not be able to see him, or touch him...

"I shall have my few belongings packed and ready," he said. "We can take Snowflake?"

She nodded. "Until New Year's, then, my lady," he said, pressing a kiss to my hand that would have been acceptable even in front of my parents, but felt deliciously wicked in this dark alcove.

And then he was gone, and I had to make my way upstairs without falling off the dizzying cloud I seemed to be floating on.

CHAPTER TWENTY-EIGHT
Avery

I re-entered the kitchen as though in a dream. The songs had changed, but the spirit was still lively, and I once again sat myself on the end of a bench and took a swig of the beer in front of me.

"Local girl, is she?" an older man asked me, and I grinned; if they'd seen who I was with, I was pretty sure their questions would have been more direct, and their faces far more shocked.

"Yeah, fairly local," I said.

"Lucky to be in love at Christmas!" he said, raising his tankard to me, and as I raised mine back, I pondered his words.

In love?

It was, surely, too quick to declare love. I wanted her, that was true - and I also wanted to save her from any hurt, or misery, or a life that she did not deserve. Was that love? I did not think I had ever been in love, and it had been something in short supply in my life - but could I envision myself being in love with her, as my wife?

Warmth flooded my chest; yes, I certainly could. Where the future had been some vague idea, with the possibility of a wife and children somewhere in the distance, it now shimmered into something more certain; something that seemed like it could well be full of love, and happiness, and warmth. Something I had never had before - but now craved more than ever.

That night I pilfered a candle from the kitchens and took it to the stables, careful to keep its flame away from the hay, and by the light of the tallow I began to whittle two gifts: one for the Viscount, who had treated me well and who I felt a little bad for leaving without a word; and one for Isabel, who had stolen my thoughts and was in danger of stealing my heart.

CHAPTER TWENTY-NINE
Isabel

"Isabel?"

I paused at the bottom of the stairs and turned to where my father stood, beneath the beautiful evergreens that decorated the door to the great hall.

"Yes, father?" I hoped my eyes did not betray that I had stayed up far later than my early departure from the festivities would suggest. I had begun to pack, hiding things under my bed that I hoped neither my maid nor my mother would notice were missing straight away. I was trying to be practical, knowing that a simpler life awaited me, and so had packed warmer, longer-lasting clothing, plus some jewellery I thought I could pawn if the need arose. In truth, I was not quite sure what I was getting myself into - even though the prospect of my future now excited me instead of scaring me.

"Will you accompany me to the library?" he said, offering his arm, and I took it, nerves rising a little. It was unusual these days for Father to have much time to speak to either of us girls alone - unless there was a pressing need.

"Sit, sit," he said, waving his arm to the green chair that sat in the corner. His own red chair was well-worn, as when he was not working, his favourite past-time was to sit and read by the fireplace. Grace had followed in his footsteps, and was often found hidden in a corner with a book - especially when she was supposed to be practising her needlework!

"Are you enjoying the festivities?" he asked, a smile on his lips, and my nerves calmed a little.

I nodded; "Indeed. The house looks beautiful, and I look forward to the play on Twelfth Night!"

"It has been a spectacular season, so far," he said. "And your betrothal to Lord Lisle - I wanted to tell you how proud I am of you making such a good match. This opportunity - well, I'm sure I don't need to tell you what it means to the family. Your mother and I, we are older, and an invitation to court would be pleasant, but not essential. But for your sister..." He sighed, and looked out of the window. "She likes to go against tradition, as I'm sure you know, but she will wish to marry well, and your marriage will ensure she has her pick of eligible men. Why, perhaps a Duke!"

My heart had fallen so low in my chest I thought it was a wonder it could still beat. Each word he said was like a knife to my heart, and yet he kept saying them with a smile on his face, and I had no defence to offer.

He did not seem to notice that I had no words in response, and so he continued. "I'm sure I am not remiss in saying that Lord Lisle might not have been your first choice, and of course he is somewhat older than you. But he will give you a comfortable life, I am sure, and the opportunities it will open for our whole family - and your children - cannot be denied."

I nodded, and swallowed, my mouth suddenly as dry as parchment.

"Do..." I began, not completely sure where my sentence was heading. "Do you think he's a good man?"

He nodded, not pausing to think. "Of course! Would King Henry himself invite a man to his table who was not a good man?"

My thoughts on that seemed better kept inside my head.

"Anyway," he said, clearly keen to move on to the next task of his day. "I just wanted to let you know how happy your mother and I are about this match. We'll have the betrothal on Twelfth Night, and then a sumptuous wedding feast a month or two later, yes?"

I nodded, not really sure what other response I could give.

"You'll need a new gown, of course, as well as new gowns that will befit your status."

Somehow, the thought of new gowns did not excite me as it once would have done.

I left the room in a daze, barely aware of my father's polite dismissal, and forgot all about plans to break my fast. Instead I headed outdoors, feeling as though I could not breathe; the tightness of my dress suddenly felt oppressive. It was cold out, but no snow fell, and I made my way round the corner until I could not be seen by any casual passer-by.

In and out, in and out, I forced myself to breathe as I let my head catch up with the words that had been said.

I had been kidding myself.

I could not leave. I could not escape this marriage to Lord Lisle. I could not give myself to Avery…

My family needed this. They were counting on me. And how could I be so selfish as to think of my happiness above that of my whole family?

As the tears began to run down my cheeks, I knew the answer; I could not.

But my heart was shattering at the thought of the future I faced.

❖ ❖ ❖

I was thankful that the men had gone hunting, and that I had opted to stay home. I had never been a big fan of the hunt, although I loved to ride, and the thought of seeing Lord Lisle astride a horse once more was enough to make me sure of my decision.

It had been a good choice, for I needed the time to think. After I had washed my face and checked in the looking glass that my morning tears were not too obvious, I joined most of the womenfolk of the party in my mother's sitting room. They smiled as I entered and continue with their pursuits; one was drawing a Christmas scene, another played the lute, and my mother and sister were sewing. That was my plan, for I still had not completed all of my New Year's gifts. I supposed my mind had been elsewhere, but it would not do to snub anyone and forget their gift.

In my mind Avery's image swam, and I wondered if I could give him a gift. If I was going to go back on my word, the least I could do was give him a gift...

The thought of never seeing him again caused an ache I had never known, and I gasped as I sank the needle into my thumb. Quickly, I threw the sampler on the floor, afraid to ruin it with the blood which flowed, and a flurry of women clucked around me.

"Here," Grace said, quick with a discarded piece of linen which she wrapped around the wound to stop the blood.

"I'm fine," I reassured them all. "I'm just sorry to have disturbed you!"

They assured me it was fine, and as they dispersed I caught my sister's eye in thanks.

"It's not like you to be so clumsy," mother said, the unspoken truth - that it was normally Grace who managed to prick herself when sewing, or rip her fabric, or knot the thread - hanging in the air around us. "Are you feeling well? You retired early last night."

I nodded, avoiding her gaze, and returned to my work - an embroidered handkerchief for Father. "I had a headache," I said. "I am well now, thank you."

She shifted closer to me, and spoke so not even Grace could hear. "If it is nerves about your wedding… fear not. I will ensure you know what is expected of you before you go to the marriage bed."

I blushed, shocked at the words Mother was saying and the image that came to my head. The image of Avery, and that barn, and the fact that I was fairly sure I had come quite close to giving myself over to the mysteries of the marriage bed before any such marriage had taken place.

I was not thinking of Lord Lisle, although luckily my mother did not know that.

"It is only natural," she said, her voice barely audible, "for you to be apprehensive, but try not to dwell on it." She patted my hand, and moved back to her sewing as if the shocking words had never passed her lips.

For a while I sat completely still, not sure my mind was clear enough to continue to sew without risk of further injury. I knew my sister was watching me closely, and was sure she had noticed my odd behaviour, but I could not think on that now.

Could there be another way out?

Perhaps, if I found someone excellent to marry my sister, I would not need to marry Lord Lisle. Someone she loved, of course - I would not sacrifice her in my place. If I could postpone my betrothal, and find her someone myself... well, then surely my parents would be far less concerned with whomever I chose to marry?

As the kernel of an idea began to form in my

head, I knew I must go to Avery when I could sneak away. I needed to tell him we could not be together now - but possibly in the future it would be so.

I needed to believe it was a possibility - because the other alternative did not bear thinking about.

CHAPTER THIRTY

Avery

It was odd, to not be working from dawn until dusk as usual, but that was the festive period. I spent the morning putting Shadow through his paces, knowing that the Viscount would want him for the hunt in the afternoon. I wondered if I would see Isabel in the stables, although I did not think the women were joining the hunt. And I was right; once the stables had emptied of the men preparing to find a deer or two, Snowflake still stood in her stall, and I found myself sad at the missed opportunity of a smile, or a furtive touching of hands.

I smiled, and shook my head; there was plenty of time. Time to get to know each other, properly, time to spend alone, time to see how a marriage between two people who barely knew each other would work out.

But then... she barely knew Lord Lisle either. And the chemistry between us was undeniable...

Once the thundering of hooves was in the distance, I decided to explore the countryside around me, making use of the free time. I was sure Isabel was busy with whatever the ladies were doing today, and sitting around wondering if I might be able to steal a kiss was not going to do either of us any good. We still had the New Year's Eve feast to attend, without raising suspicion, and I needed to finish gifts for my employer, as well as Mr Radcliffe, as the host. And Isabel... I wanted to present something to her, too, even if I could never offer anything of much value.

But I had offered her my name, and my protection.

I wondered if one day I could offer my heart. As I wandered into the woods, my whittling tools in the pocket of the warm coat Isabel had gifted me, I pondered the fact that my heart had always been my own; with no parents I remembered, I had never felt that love for them, and my brother had succumbed to the plague when I was so young, I barely remembered the love I had felt for him. There had never been anyone else in my life I had been close enough to for love to develop. I had known a couple of women, over the years, but that was certainly not love, for me or them.

Was this different?

In the clearing ahead, surrounded by snow and peaceful silence, was a tree stump, and it made a perfect seat.

Of course it was different. I had offered marriage. I had offered everything I had - including my hopes and dreams for the future, even if she knew little of them - to Isabel Radcliffe, and that had never happened before. As innocent as she was, I was fairly confident that she would have given in to the overwhelming desire between the two of us without a marriage proposal. And so I knew it was not just lust driving me, but something more.

Something that, one day, I thought could well be love.

I took out my knife, and several pieces of wood I had found while out riding, and let my thoughts take over as the gifts began to take shape.

CHAPTER THIRTY-ONE

Isabel

Dinner seemed like it would never end, especially with Lord Lisle so excited about the kill he had secured. I was not sure how, with his poor horsemanship, he had stayed astride long enough to snare a deer, but I knew that was uncharitable, and most definitely not something I could say out loud.

"The New Year's feast will be magnificent!" my father was saying, and I smiled in an attempt to agree. Tomorrow we would exchange our New Year's gifts, and dance until the birds were almost awake. And then in only a few short days it would be Twelfth Night, and I would be betrothed to Lord Lisle…

No. I would find a way to delay, and then find someone incredibly eligible for Grace to marry. It was the only way - the only way everyone could be happy. For as much as I wanted to give my family everything they wished for, surely it could not only come at the expense of my own happily ever after?

"I cannot wait," Grace said, tucking in to her pheasant with enthusiasm.

"You just like receiving gifts," I teased, but she smiled back and - thankfully - refrained from sticking out her tongue, which she was wont to do.

"I am looking forward to giving you your New Year's gift, Isabel," Lord Lisle said next to me, and I felt the hairs on my arms and neck prickle. Why did the man have to make me feel so uncomfortable? I did not like the way my name sounded on his lips, either, and I had to push Avery from my mind - not for the first time that night.

I lowered my gaze, already well-practiced at hiding my emotions from him. "That is very generous of you, my lord."

"Well, I think I can afford to be generous to my wife-to-be," he said, patting my arm with a large hand. The words caught the attention of the other guests, who so far had at not known, or at least pretended not to know of the planned betrothal, and I felt my heart drop in horror.

This public acknowledgment felt as good as wedding band on my finger. The noose around my neck that was getting harder and harder to escape.

"Congratulations!" was called several times, and I tried to smile, struggling to raise my eyes and meet all of those that were staring back at me. Were any wondering what sort of marriage we could have? Why we were marrying when we were so clearly unsuited?

Of course not. People married for status and money all the time; there was no reason I should be any different.

"They shall be betrothed on Twelfth Night," I heard mother tell the young Elizabeth, and my heart constricted in panic. I wanted to close my eyes and pretend none of it were happening, but I was too old for such fairy tales.

What a mess I had got myself in.

◆ ◆ ◆

"Don't leave me," I muttered to Grace, as the evening drew to a close. I was fairly sure if Lord Lisle found me alone, he would try to kiss me - and that was something I could not handle tonight. I already had to tell Avery our plan could not work, with the memory of his kisses burnt into my soul; I could not cope with the feel of Lord Lisle's lips against mine.

For once, Grace did not question me, but stayed by my side as everyone said good night, having sung and played cards and talked until they were ready for slumber.

"My lady," Lord Lisle said, tipping me a bow, and I bobbed a curtsy but did not let go of Grace's arm.

"Good night, my lord," I said, and he only lingered a moment before obviously deciding his luck would not be in tonight.

"Thank you," I whispered as we mounted the stairs together - although, as soon as the house was quiet, I planned to sneak out to speak with Avery. I could not bear the burden of these words for the whole night; I needed to speak with him before I had a hope of sleeping.

"I think you're keeping secrets from me," she said, as we reached my bedchamber.

I was going to deny it, but thought better; after all, she spoke the truth. "It's for your own good," I reassured her.

"I'm not a child, you know," she said, pouting in a way that almost made me laugh, and did indeed look very childish. "You can tell me."

I reached out to touch my fingers to her dark hair, which had delicate braids woven through it. "Thank you, Gracie. I cannot now… but I appreciate you being here for me. Good night."

She nodded, and although I doubted I had appeased her, she went to bed without a fuss - as I began the interminable wait for it to be safe to sneak outside.

◆ ◆ ◆

The house had been silent for a long while when I eventually moved to leave it. If I were honest, I was putting off this moment of heartbreak for as long as I could - and no creaks or coughs had been heard for a long time now. I wore my nightgown, for Hettie would have been suspicious if I had not dressed for bed, but wrapped a thick cloak around myself, both for heat and propriety's sake.

The snow was falling prettily onto the tree tops and the blanketed floor, and my footprints disappeared almost as soon as I had made them. I ran across the moonlit grounds, knowing if I thought about what I was doing, I might back out. How often I had felt that this week - and yet for so many different reasons.

There was a magic in the air that spoke of Christmas and new beginnings, and it almost seemed cruel, given my current situation. I wondered, as I took one last steadying breath and crossed the threshold, whether I would ever be able to think of Christmas without thinking of these days of magic and heartbreak.

Without the light of the moon, it was pitch

black, and the silence suggested he was asleep. I had presumed he would be, but this conversation needed to be had immediately, and there was no way of me being here with him while everyone was awake - and so we would both have to sacrifice our sleep.

CHAPTER THIRTY-TWO

Avery

"Avery? Avery?" My eyes flickered open, registering that it was still dark and that, quite possibly, not much time had passed since I had finally found sleep. What had woken me? Footsteps below me caused me to sit up so fast my head span, and then I heard it again.

"Avery?" Her voice, gentle, shaking slightly, unmistakably her.

"Isabel." It wasn't a question, merely an acknowledgment that I had heard her. I hurried down the ladder, not thinking about the fact that I wore only a thin shirt and breeches, and as my eyes adjusted, I made out her figure stood just inside the doorway, a silhouette in the moon's light that bathed the snowy ground outside.

I reached out, taking her hands in mine almost automatically, feeling warm at the thought of her being here, just the two of us again. Thoughts of our last kiss flooded my mind and I wondered how sensible it was for her to be here. Could we both control our emotions, our bodies, until we were legally wed? I was not entirely convinced.

"I need to talk to you," she said, and something in her voice warned me that I might not like the words I was about to hear. "Can- can we sit?"

I nodded, although I wasn't sure she could see me, and led her to the hay bales we had sat on previously. I was about to offer to find a candle to light, but she began to speak and I let the words fill the darkness without interruption.

"My father spoke with me today," she said, her voice wobbling a little. "And he told me - he told me how important this marriage is. How much we need it as a family, how great it will be for Grace, how - how proud of me he is." She was crying, I was sure, and as my fingers moved to her face I felt the hot, salty tears falling, and wished there was something I could say to stop them.

Had she been talked out of marrying me without anyone even knowing of our plan?

"What are you saying, Isabel?" I said, my words harsher than I meant them to be, my heart constricting in my chest.

"All day," she said, resting her cheek against my hand. "All day I have been trying to come up with a plan, a plan that can make everyone happy. And I think I have - but we cannot run away before Twelfth Night."

I withdrew my hand, feeling the cold air swirling around us as I lost the warmth of that connection. "So you'll be betrothed to Lord Lisle?" The words tasted bitter as they left my lips, but I always liked to know the plan, to know where I stood - no matter how painful.

"No!" She grabbed my face in both of her hands, and I gasped at the unexpected contact, the desire that having her soft, warm hands on my body could provoke. "No. I will delay - I will stall. Somehow. And I will find my sister an eligible match - someone she'll be happy with, as well as my parents, and then who I marry won't matter. And then…" Her breath hitched, and both of us moved closer without noticing. "And then," she whispered, our lips almost touching, "We can marry. If… if you'll still have me."

I lifted my hand to hold hers against my cheek. "If they won't care who you marry," I said, cursing myself for saying words that could take away the happy future I had pictured; "Will you still want to marry me?"

She didn't answer, well, not in words, but she closed the gap between our mouths and pressed her lips to mine with an intensity that made me groan. One hand remained on the side of my face, and as our lips danced together, our bodies moved closer, craving warmth in the cold, cold night. I let my tongue touch her lips and they opened without question, deepening the kiss with a trust and ferocity that made me sure my concerns about our self-control were definitely well-founded.

"If you'll have me, Avery," she said, her breath uneven, "yes, once I am free to, I will gladly marry you."

I could imagine her cheeks flushing red, although the darkness prohibited me from seeing, and while this delay made my heart nervous that everything would fall through, I took courage from her passionate words.

"I'd marry you tomorrow," I told her, surprising myself with how true the words were. "And I'll wait until you are ready - although I can't lie and say I'm not disappointed that the plan has changed."

❖ ❖ ❖

My heart swelled at his words. He had offered to marry me to save me from a marriage to Lord Lisle - but the fact that he still wanted to marry me if that weren't hanging over our heads felt like something so much more.

Had he imagined our futures, like I had? Was he anticipating our wedding night, like I was?

Tears of frustration welled in my eyes at the thought of all that being postponed, but then his lips were on mine again and I tried to enjoy it all, tried to give myself to the moment and not worry about how I was going to achieve the task I had set myself. Find my sister a husband, of good breeding, whom she wanted to marry - how hard could it be?

A little voice in my head told me it would be far harder than I thought, but I pushed it away and for a few moments gave my body over to the feeling of his hands on my waist, his tongue against mine, his hips pressing against me as we vented our shared frustrations.

CHAPTER THIRTY-THREE
Isabel

Sleep took a long time to come that night, even with the late hour I had finally gone to bed, and when it eventually arrived my dreams were a whirl of colours and faces, making me feel nervous and on edge but with no real knowledge of why. When the sun streaming through the windows woke me up, I felt as though I'd barely had an hour of full sleep, but dragged myself up for the day ahead of me. The New Year's feast was tonight, and so sleep was a long way off.

As I glanced in the looking glass and saw my eyes, red from tears shed the previous night and ringed with black circles from the lack of sleep, I thought I would probably have to take a nap if I were to make it through the festivities. I needed to pretend to be happy; I needed to see if I could find a husband for Grace. Tonight was as good a time as any to start looking - a few local gentlemen who had not stayed for the whole festive period would be attending the ball, and perhaps one would take her fancy.

I also needed to figure out how to postpone my betrothal. Once the words were said and witnessed between us, it did not matter that the marriage had not taken place - I would be unable to marry anyone else. And while the life of a spinster was certainly more appealing than life spent as Lady Lisle, now that I had glimpsed a future where I thought I could be happy, I did not want to lose it.

As Hettie arrived to help me dress and brush out my hair, I let my thoughts wander. She did not comment on my tired eyes, and I was thankful; it was hard to keep track of lies. How had Avery become such an important part of my life in eight short days? When I closed my eyes I saw his smile, his full lips that felt so heavenly on mine, his broad hands that were calloused from working hard but somehow so gentle on my waist. I saw his thighs as he sat astride Shadow, and I blushed at the thought of how his body made me feel.

But I also saw a simple life; I saw a small cottage, plain dresses and children running in and out. I saw Christmas decorations that were rustic and made with love and a husband coming home at the end of the day with a warm kiss and tender words.

It was not a fancy life. It was not a life full of rich food and fine clothes and the prospect of being at court - a life I had always thought I wanted. A life I had been told to chase, a life I thought would make me happy.

No, it was a quiet life, with herbs growing in the garden and early nights in front of a fire. It was a life that I had never known I wanted - and somehow now it had been in my grasp, it was all I could dream of.

A life with Avery; a life where I felt safe, and wanted, and loved. A life where the drama of court and the gossip of Henry taking a new wife would not affect me.

My eyes shone brightly with tears and the hope of tomorrow, and as they met Hettie's in the glass I smiled. She smiled back, keeping any questions to herself, and I let the image in my mind go, for now. Now that I knew what I wanted, my heart felt exposed to the harsh outside world, and I had to push thoughts that my plan might fail away, else the panic of losing it all would engulf me.

◆ ◆ ◆

It was early enough that I was sure Mother would still be in her sitting room, and when I knocked I heard her voice calling for me to enter. She smiled as she saw me, and I felt my heart jolt a little about the deception I had planned, even if I had put it off for now.

"Isabel, dear, good morning."

"Good morning Mother," I said, leaning over to press a kiss to her cheek before taking seat opposite her. She did not seem to be occupied by anything except looking out of the window, and so I did not think I would be disturbing her with my visit.

"I wanted to talk to you..." I said, nerves building, "About my betrothal."

"Oh?" Thankfully she did not try to talk to me about the mysteries of the marital bedchamber; as interested as I was to hear them, I was also embarrassed, and this morning's conversation was going to be difficult enough.

"I was thinking, it might be best if we... postponed it, a little, until later in the year. What with how much effort and money has been put into the Christmas celebrations, I thought it might be better to...wait."

Mother looked at me for a few moments, clearly weighing up my words, before answering. My foot tapped beneath the chair, an unladylike trait that Mother would have normally commented on - but not today.

"Your betrothal won't cost anything, dear, and then when your marriage follows, well, your father is more than happy to spend money on ensuring you are rightly prepared for life as a lady."

"But if we put it off, just a few months, I could stay here with you, I could help find Grace a husband, I could-"

"Isabel. Grace cannot be married until you are, you know there are rules to be followed. And, if I may speak frankly, and with no chance of these words leaving this room - well, Lord Lisle is not a young man. He is older than your father, and I'm sure that is not to your taste, but these things must be borne. Who knows when the Good Lord may call him to be with him, and then you will be in a fine mess if you were not legally married. No, Isabel, your betrothal must be this week, before he leaves, and your wedding not long after."

My words were falling on deaf ears and even as I struggled for another argument, I knew they would all be dismissed. My heart felt like it was breaking in two as I tried one last-ditch attempt.

"You married for love, Mother," I said in a quiet voice. "Didn't you?"

A small smile graced her lips, but her eyes were guarded, and I held little hope that my words would make a difference.

"I did. But I was not a woman of wealth, like you, and I was the youngest sister. Things are different now - and that is the way it must be. You may well come to have great affection for Lord Lisle, once you are married."

That seemed as likely to me as King Henry turning up for dinner, but I politely excused myself and ran to my room, tears falling from my eyes, realising now what I had refused to accept before:

There was no hope.

I could leave with Avery, and break my family's hearts and chances for success.

I could stay and be married to Lord Lisle within the month.

Neither felt like an option I could take. With more force than necessary, I wrenched open my bedroom door and slammed it behind me, tears obscuring my vision. I pulled my bag from under my bed and tipped the contents out, knowing they would no longer be needed. Simple dresses and jewels to pawn - not necessary for Lady Lisle. I would spend my life caged in fancy dresses, the property of a man who did not love nor respect me.

And my heart was shattered upon the floor.

I did not hear a knock, but I whirled around to find Grace standing there, her eyes wide as she took in the scene.

"Isabel, what's the matter?"

"Nothing," I snapped, knowing it was not her fault but struggling to keep my emotions locked away.

She closed the door behind her and sat herself on my bed, amongst the mess of clothes and jewellery I had emptied out.

"I could hear you slamming the door from downstairs," she said, with a shrug. "So I don't believe that."

I sighed, and sank into a wooden chair by the window. "It's complicated."

"Is it about your wedding?"

I nodded.

"I don't think you should marry him, Isabel," she said, reaching out to smooth the hem of a simple blue dress in front of her. "No, listen - he's so old, and I don't even think he's very nice. I know he's a *lord,*" she rolled her eyes at the word, and despite my current state of anguish I had to bite back a laugh. "But you will be with him for the rest of - well, the rest of his life, certainly." Well, I knew I could always rely on Grace to be direct.

"I-" How much could I tell her? I looked at her innocent face and knew I would never want to burden her with the fact that one of the main reasons I needed to marry Lord Lisle was so she herself could be settled well. It wasn't her fault, after all - and I knew she would say that it didn't matter, that I should follow my own heart - but she was young, and she could not yet understand what implications that might have.

Feeling once again like I was struggling to breathe, I pushed the window open and took a few deep breaths of the icy air. "I thought I had a plan. I thought I could get out of it... but I can't."

"A plan to marry someone else?"

How could she know? I panicked a little; if it were obvious to her, was it obvious to everyone else? But no, surely Mother or Father would have said something.

"Perhaps."

She smiled knowingly, and I took several deep breaths.

"Is it Avery? I've seen the way he looks at you, and the way you look at him..."

I groaned. "Is it that obvious?" I said in a whisper, and Grace quickly shook her head.

"No, it's just - well, I saw you kiss under the kissing bough, so I guess I've been watching! So you do want to marry him?"

I avoided her gaze. "I thought... I thought I might. But it's impossible."

"Why? It's so romantic!"

"Romance isn't enough!" I almost shouted, then remembered we were not the only occupants of the house. I lowered my voice. "He is of low birth, he has no money, no assets, no hope of anything better in his future than being a farmer - why on earth would I marry him?" I was laying it on thick in order to dissuade my sister of the notion. I did not want to have to reveal the truth; that if I did marry him, it might ruin her prospects, and those of the whole family.

Even though I knew I did not mean them, the words burnt as they left my lips, leaving a foul taste in my mouth, and I fought to hold back tears.

"But I've seen the electricity between you two!" Grace exclaimed, wrapped up in the fairytale of it all as she so often was. "Surely-"

"No, Grace. I cannot marry him. I must marry Lord Lisle - he has a title, and with my wealth, we will make a powerful alliance. You shall be married soon, too, I'm sure."

She crossed her arms over her chest in a fit of pique. "I shall never marry someone I don't like, someone I don't respect."

"You don't know what you'll do," I snapped back, turning to the window. "I will see you at dinner."

She took the dismissal, and as soon as I heard the door close I allowed myself to sink to the floor, the tears spilling hard and fast as I gave up the attempt to control them.

CHAPTER THIRTY-FOUR

Avery

"He is of low birth, he has no money, no assets, no hope of anything better in his future than being a farmer - why on earth would I marry him?"

My heart faltered as I heard the words, in that voice that I would have recognised anywhere. They floated from the window as though they were innocent thoughts, and not knives sent to pierce my heart.

Why would she want to marry me?

I had asked myself the same thing many times over - and here she was giving every reason I could have thought of. My dreams of becoming a yeoman farmer suddenly seemed small and insignificant, my lack of money and a title the only thing to define me. I had thought those things myself - but I had not heard them said, and I was shocked at just how much they hurt.

I had worried her plan to get out of marrying Lord Lisle would not work - but I had not realised that she did not *want* to get out of it.

I heard her declare that she would marry him, that he had a title, and then I turned on my heel and walked back to the stables. Without thinking, I jumped upon Shadow, not bothering with a saddle, and kicked my heels until we were flying through the door, across the snowy woodland and away to find some place where I could not be hurt.

I always knew I came from nothing, but I had never felt ashamed about it. I had always known she was destined for greater things - and yet when she had accepted my hand, I had trusted her.

What a fool I had been.

❖ ❖ ❖

With no-one expecting me, and with no plan that I knew of for the Viscount to go riding, I rode hard and fast, through the local village, through open fields and along a poorly maintained road, until I reached something I had never seen before, something I did not even know was within an hour's ride.

The sea.

With a childhood spent in London, and working further North for the Viscount, it had never been something I had happened upon - and I'd never had any great desire to make the effort to visit a beach and see the glittering ocean.

I had not realised what I had been missing.

I dismounted, telling Shadow I would be back before slipping him a carrot, and picked my way across pebbles and stones and sand until I reached the water's edge. Despite my blood running warm, I regretted not wearing the thick coat. The wind seemed colder here, with a bite I could not escape, and yet I revelled in the fact that it stopped me thinking of those words that Isabel had spoken. Who had she said them to? What else had she said? Despite the intensity of my ride here, I had not been able to force the questions from my mind, and yet the cold stopped them for a moment.

I removed my shoes and netherhose, feeling the sand crunch between my toes. The endless water stretched before me, making everything seem insignificant. I took two steps in and shouted, both in shock at the temperature and in delight at the sensation of the icy water. I could swim, if I chose, but even in my anguish I knew that swimming in rough, cold seas was not a sensible plan. I did not want to die; I had a life to lead.

A life that seemed very empty and cold compared with yesterday, but a life none the less. If she thought so little of me, then that was her choice. I should have known better than to let her into my heart, than to expect love from someone like her. I was a fool, and I would never let myself be fooled again, I vowed, as my shirt was sprayed by the salty waves.

Perhaps love was out there, but for me, I knew it was not. No, I would plan, I would even possibly marry one day - but love could not be part of the equation. This first foray into the possibility of love had taught me that; if this pain, after so few days, was anything to go by, then it just was not worth it.

I did not know how long I spent, looking out to sea and contemplating the mistakes I had made, but when I realised I was losing the feeling in my extremities, I knew it was time to head back. I rode Shadow just as hard home, eager to warm up and get something to eat, and put this entire day behind me. Tonight was the New Year's Eve feast and dance, which I knew I would have to attend, and gifts would be exchanged. The Viscount had planned to stay all the way until Twelfth Night, feeling the journey was not warranted without a decent length stay, and so I would have five more days to avoid seeing Isabel before I could leave.

It was strange, how leaving this place could make me feel like I was leaving something behind. I had never planned to leave the Viscount's service, and yet somehow an idea had been put into motion that would involve me never returning to the place I had called home for the last couple of years. And now I was reverting to my original intentions - and yet my feelings had changed so completely.

I tended to Shadow before heading in for some warmth, whispering soft words of thanks to him for the ride. Then, rubbing my hands together to try to regain some feeling, I headed for the kitchen, hoping some of the lunch would be left. I was a little late for the meal, but the cook was pleasant and generally seemed happy to help.

The warmth of the fireplace hit me as I entered and I stood before it for a few moments, feeling the tingle of pain as the sensation returned to my fingertips.

"You'll be ill," one of the maids said as she walked past me. "Your lips are blue! Have you been out in this cold dressed like that?" She tutted, but when she reappeared she held a bowl of steaming soup, a hunk of break and a thick cloak.

"Here," she said, putting it down on the end of the table that was nearest the fire. "Get that inside you. You don't want to miss out on the gifts tonight!"

I thanked her, and as she walked away I watched her hips sway. She was pretty, with dark curly hair and red lips that looked like they were well-practiced in smiling. But despite her pleasing looks I felt nothing - nothing but gratitude for the warm soup, which I ate greedily as I pushed thoughts of Isabel from my head.

I did not want to go to the feast tonight - but the Viscount would, as tradition dictated, have a gift for me, and I a gift for him. I needed his patronage; I planned to work for him for the next few years, before trying to set out on my own. While Isabel may have found my dreams small, I reminded myself that all I was aiming for was what would make me happy - and it was a big dream to me. I tried not to care what she thought - although I was failing miserably at that.

CHAPTER THIRTY-FIVE

Isabel

The effort it was taking not to cry was making it difficult to make small talk with Hettie as she braided my hair, and helped me into the blue dress I had chosen for this evening. I barely noticed how I looked, knowing that everything had changed and I had no way out of the prison I was heading for. At occasional moments I wondered if I could go to Avery, if he might have some idea - but then I dismissed the thought. At some point I would have to tell him that hope was lost - but I could not bring myself to do it today, when everyone was so excited about the gifts, the food, the drinking, the dancing.

Would I ever be able to look at Christmas in the same way? I had always loved it, but now I thought I would always look back on this time with Avery with a broken heart. I would look at my last few weeks of freedom and see everything I had lost - and how could Christmas ever hold the same magic after that?

"You look beautiful, Mistress Isabel," Hettie said, and I managed to smile and thank her. I felt ugly from the words I had spoken to my sister earlier, from the dark thoughts that filled my head, but that was not her fault. She had done wonders, and despite my tired eyes and grimacing face, the image that looked back at me from the mirror was indeed beautiful. I was sure Lord Lisle would love her - even if he would never know her properly.

"Thank you," I said, forcing the smile to remain on my face. "Are you looking forward to the feast this evening?"

She smiled, and nodded. "We all are!"

How I wished I could feel the same.

Grace did not smile at me as we descended the stairs together, and I felt another wrench in my heart that I had damaged my relationship with my little sister. There was time, I told myself, to fix it before I would leave this home to live with Lord Lisle. There had to be.

"You look beautiful," I said. I knew it was a gown from the previous year, and felt guilty that I had been given so many new dresses while she wore old ones - but she did look beautiful in it. The green set off her eyes and her hair seemed to shimmer in the candlelight.

"Thank you," she said, but there was still no smile as we took our seats together at the front of the great hall, beside mother and father.

They beamed as the servants lined up, keen to give us gifts and receive gifts in return. In practice, the gifts we gave far outvalued the gifts we were given, but the thought that had gone into some of the presents touched my heart. Mostly Father and Mother gave and received the gifts, but for Hettie, who spent most of her time with me, I had a new gown, and her enthusiastic response made my smile far more genuine.

"For you, Mistress Isabel," she said, and I opened the box to find beautifully decorated comfits.

"Thank you, Hettie - these look incredible!"

Her smiled broadened, and it was only as she stepped away that I noticed who was speaking to my father. My breath hitched as Avery's warm brown eyes touched upon me, before they flicked back to my father, who he was presenting with our family crest, whittled into a piece of oak.

"This is a fine gift, young man," Father was saying, and I could see the pride in his eyes. Our ascension, our need of a family crest - that was so important to him, and so this gift was surely one he would cherish. How like Avery to figure out what someone might want - even if it was someone he barely knew.

"My lord," he said, dipping his head so his dark hair fell forwards, and then moving away. My eyes followed him but he did not show any sign of noticing me. Was he trying to keep up the pretense? Or did he somehow know that I could no longer keep my word and marry him?

My staring was interrupted by a gift being pressed into my hands, and when I looked up, Lord Lisle loomed over me, a smile on his lips, his cheeks red from the wine he had consumed.

"Happy New Year," he said, watching as I opened the ribbon tying the box closed. Inside was a jewel, far bigger than anything I had ever owned. It was too big to be pretty, but it must have been worth a fair sum.

"Thank you," I said, not able to force his first name through my lips. "You are too generous. It is very impressive."

"I acquired it recently, and wished to show my wife-to-be how important she is." I wished his words could cause a flutter in my stomach of anything that was not panic - but alas, they did not.

I reached behind me for the gift I had for him, and he grinned as he tore it open. "Wonderful, thank you," he said, placing the handkerchiefs in his pocket without even noticing the careful embroidery of his initials on every one.

I hid a sigh, and turned to hand gifts to the rest of my family. For Father, a similar set of handkerchiefs; for my mother and sister, matching velvet purses I had sewn myself.

My gift from Grace was given without any words, and when I opened it I too was speechless, although not through anger. Her skill with a paintbrush had long been known, but this portrait of our family, which must have been drawn from memory since we had partaken in no sitting, was exquisite.

"Grace!" I exclaimed, as I ran my fingers over the textured paint, noticing the slight smile on my lips in the image; a shoelace undone on Grace's left foot; the stern, solid expression on Father's face; and the warmth that somehow radiated from Mother, even as her expression was carefully schooled to look serious. "This is beyond compare. This is-" A tear came to my eye at the thought of leaving them, and of having this to look upon whenever I felt homesick. "This is a wonderful gift."

I reached out to squeeze her hand and was gratified that she did not try to withdraw it. There was no time to embrace, but I hoped that the divide between us might be bridged.

I thanked Mother and Father for the beautiful new sleeves they had presented me with, and wondered whether I would be able to give Avery the gift I had worked on for him by the light of a candle in my bedroom. I could not do it publicly, of course, for what reason would I have to give the Viscount's groom a gift? But I had been unable to stop myself from making him a token, and the cap I had knitted and lined with fur would surely make a life spent in the cold more pleasant.

I toyed with the idea of sneaking out to give it to him that night, but the knowledge of what I must tell him weighed heavy on my heart, and I let the notion slip. For now I must pretend to be merry, must dance and feast, and when the door to my bedchamber closed - only then could I truly grieve what I had lost.

CHAPTER THIRTY-SIX

Avery

I watched her dance, I watched her smile, I watched her hold her sister's hands and share the wassail bowl. Did she not realise the pain she had caused?

Of course not. I was some temporary distraction, who had no more right to a place on her mind that the rest of the staff who served her.

Her New Year's gift burnt a hole in my pocket, but I could not give it to her. I had already known when I made it that I would have to give it to her secretly - but I had brought it with me for reasons that were still a mystery, even to me. The carving of Snowflake onto a small wooden token had taken me longer than all the other gifts combined, but I had spent the hours joyfully planning a life together that could now no longer be.

Out of the corner of my eye I saw the Viscount approach me, and I stood straighter, trying to look a little less glum.

"Happy New Year, my lord," I said, bowing my head briefly and handing him a small wrapped parcel. His gnarled fingers took a moment to open it, but he gave a rare smile when he saw the carved hunting whistle.

"Thank you, Avery. A fine piece of work." He handed me a parcel, heavy and oddly shaped. I thanked him before opening it, and was pleased to find a pair of new boots, lined with fur.

He disappeared before I had a chance to say any more, and I decided to head to the stable to safely stow them. They looked warm and comfortable and would replace my heavily repaired shoes - and I wondered if the Viscount had noticed I was in need of them.

CHAPTER THIRTY-SEVEN

Isabel

Without stopping to weigh up my options, I followed him as I saw him leave the great hall, out into the snow. I was tempted to call out, but I did not know who might be around, and so I waited until I reached the stables, just a moment or two behind him.

"Avery," I said, not wanting to make him jump. As he turned, the look he gave me stopped me in my tracks. The kindness, the longing, the sparkle I was used to seeing in his eyes - all of it gone. How could that be? I had not even told him what I must yet.

"What do you want, Isabel?" he asked, turning away to stow some boots in his leather satchel.

"I-I-" I stuttered out the words, unsure as to the reason for his icy demeanour. "I wanted to give you your present," I eventually said, my hand shaking a little as I passed him the parcel. He took it without meeting my eye, and placed it on the bench behind him.

"Thank you," he said, and when the silence dragged on I could not stop myself from asking. I had to know why he suddenly could not look at me - even if I was afraid that what I had to tell him would only solidify the feeling.

"Has something happened?" I finally asked.

"No," he said curtly, and for a moment I though he was not going to say another word. Then he met my eyes, just for a second, before going back to examining the straw beneath us. "This - this just can't work. We both know it. We both know we cannot continue like this."

I took a sharp breath, shocked at his words even though I could not deny them. I wanted to ask why, how he knew, what he knew - but what would that help? We could not be together - that was the truth.

I hung my head, feeling the tears welling and the pain of my broken heart radiating through my chest. "I know," I whispered, wishing I could take his hand, wishing he would hold me, but knowing that would not help in the long run. "How I wish it weren't true, but it is."

"Don't lie to me," he said softly, and my head whipped up at that, for I did not think I had ever lied to him, not in the short time I had known him.

"What-"

"Ah, there you are! What a funny time to go to the stables!" His voice sounded jovial, but when I turned to see Lord Lisle, larger than life in the stable doorway, his eyes did not match his voice.

Thankfully, there was a respectable distance between Avery and I - but I was sure my tears were obvious to anyone.

"I wanted to make sure Snowflake was being well taken care of," I lied, trying to make my words sound confident. "The weather feels cooler, and she has a delicate temperament."

"All you think about is that horse!" he said, and I thought that rather unfair. He did not know what I thought about - although there was probably a blessing in that.

He offered his arm, and I had no choice but to accept it. "Make sure you take care of the horse, since it's so important to Mistress Isabel," he said to Avery, and I could not tell him that Avery did not work for us, or that it was not his job to see to Snowflake.

"Of course, *my lord*," Avery said, and as he bowed overly low, I saw a blackness in his eyes that made me shiver.

"Come," Lord Lisle said, turning abruptly. "We must get you back to the house before you freeze. No place for a lady."

I followed him because there was nothing else I could do - and I could not even risk a glance back at Avery. My head was confused, my heart broken, and a million questions plagued me. But all of that would have to be dealt with later - for right now, I had to make sure Lord Lisle was not suspicious.

He stopped just before we entered through the stone archway, his hand on my arm, tighter than was comfortable.

"There isn't anything I should know, is there Isabel?" he asked, his gaze holding mine, and I shook my head quickly.

"Know? Of course not, my lord." The answer was too quick, and my voice far too squeaky, but for now he seemed to accept it. He nodded, anyway, and steered me into the hall, insisting on the next dance.

Was I destined to spend the rest of my life dancing when all I wanted to do was cry?

◆ ◆ ◆

After the company tired of dancing, games were called for, and a raucous game of Hood Man Blind began. Somehow I was first, and with apprehension I allowed Grace to cover my eyes, before reaching out in the hope of catching someone quickly. Shrieks and giggles broke out whenever I came close, and the frustration of playing some stupid game when my life was in such disarray nearly brought me to tears. I reached out and snagged a dress, but it was gone before my hands could close. Then I felt my hands on a warm body, strong arms, but before I could pull off my blindfold, another set of hands were on my waist, squeezing tighter than was comfortable.

I pulled off the blindfold, and there was Lord Lisle, face ruddy and eyes slightly unfocused due to the amount of wine he had drunk.

"Well caught, Mistress Isabel," he said, indicating I should blindfold him, and as I slipped the fabric over his eyes, I looked wildly around. I was sure he was not the first person I had landed on - but there was no-one else near.

My heart sank and I moved away, not willing to be caught, and not keen to join in the revelry. I wished fervently that Lord Lisle's hands would never have to be on my body again.

◆ ◆ ◆

I knew I was a glutton for punishment as I ran through the snowy night once more. Before this Christmas, I could not remember sneaking out - and yet this week I had done so more than I could count. But that look in his eyes, the accusation of lying - even though we could not be together, I knew I could not live the rest of my life not knowing what he meant. Not knowing what had changed his plans, even if I knew what had changed mine.

I spotted him before I tried the stable. It was the glow of fire that caught my eye, and as I got closer I saw him sat in front of the flames, warming his hands and drinking a tankard of ale. I found myself fluttering with nerves as I approached, but they were different to the giddy butterflies I had felt in previous days. Tonight I did not expect a kiss that would leave me breathless, but instead a sharp rebuff - and I wasn't sure my fragile heart could take it.

He saw me before I spoke, and I heard the sigh come from his lips.

"I told you, Isabel. I told you we were done. Could you… could you please leave me alone?"

The words hurt more than I expected, an icy knife to the chest that left me struggling to breathe - and still I stepped forwards.

CHAPTER THIRTY-EIGHT

Avery

She wasn't going. Why, why, why was she not just turning and leaving? Had she not hurt me enough? I thought this afternoon would be it, I thought that I could make it through the next few days and then move on with my life. The words I had overheard this morning had sharpened and focussed my mind - but seeing her did nothing to help the pain that they had caused.

I closed my eyes, trying to focus on the heat emanating from the fire instead of what I must say. "You were right. I am not good enough for you. My birth is too low, my dreams too small, my wealth non-existent." I heard her gasp, and still I did not open my eyes. "You were right. I am not good enough for you, and I was a fool to have forgotten that."

"Why... why are you saying that?" she asked,

and I had to look then because surely she could recognise her own words being thrown back at her?

"I heard you," I said, keeping my tone as free of emotion as possible, in spite of the fact that it raged through my body, causing pain everywhere it touched. "I heard you this morning. I was stupid to think that we could overcome so many differences. You were right."

"Avery..." I did not look at her again, because I knew there was a chance it would break me, knew that her tears might once again have me declaring things I had no place declaring. "Avery, I cannot marry you," she choked out, and although I knew that already, it did not make the words any less harsh to my ears. "It is not - it is not for any of the reasons I said. I promise you that." I could hear her tears, but I did not face her, and so I could only imagine them falling into the dense snow beneath us.

"It is my duty," she said. "I must... I must do right by my family. I'm sorry."

When I opened my eyes she was gone, only the footprints in the snow left to acknowledge that she had been there.

And I was left with a dying fire, a thousand questions about what she had said and something which closely resembled a broken heart.

❖ ❖ ❖

I spent most of the night awake, staring at the black ceiling and hearing the wildlife trying to find food in the snowstorm. Occasionally one of the horses would whinny or snort, but other than that, peace and quiet reigned - and yet sleep was a long way off.

I tried not to picture the life I had been imagining since I had asked her to marry me. As upset as I was at the words she had said, at the confirmation that I was not good enough for her, I also mourned the loss of a future that had become so real in my mind. A future I now wanted…but that now felt so far out of my reach.

In my hands I turned over the circle of wood I had spent so many hours engraving, the picture of Snowflake etched in my mind as surely as it was in the wood. She had given me a gift, but I could not bring myself to give her one in return. Once she had left, I had opened it, holding the softness of the hat to my face and trying not to think about the hours it must have taken, the secretive effort she must have gone to, the thoughtfulness at giving me a gift that would protect me from the cold.

Why did she put so much effort in, just to break my heart? It made no sense, but then neither did the words she had said to me tonight, while tears fell from her eyes. None of this made sense - none of it, except the fact that I was not good enough to marry her. Wasn't that what I had always known?

Except... I turned over so forcefully the wood beneath me creaked, and sighed into the straw mattress. Except the anger building inside of me at the thought of her words told me that, maybe, I *was* good enough. I had been good enough when she had needed an escape; I was good enough when I offered her everything I had, however meagre it might be. I was good enough when we were exchanging soft kisses, when desire was overwhelming us, when I had checked on her when she had fallen from her horse.

I was good enough - but that didn't make it any less painful.

The piece of wood threatened to snap in my angry fingertips, and I dropped it on the floor next to me with a loud sigh, as I wished for time to speed up and Twelfth Night to be upon us, so I could leave this place and never return.

CHAPTER THIRTY-NINE

Isabel

"A ride will do you good," Mother insisted as she wrapped my riding cloak around me, seemingly unconcerned with the fact that I was not a willing participant. "You've seemed a little out of sorts."

That was sorely underestimating things. Several nights of little to no sleep and more crying than I had ever done in my life was taking a toll on my mood and my complexion. The idea of a ride was not helping - inevitably, I would see Avery, and after his harsh words last night I did not know if I could do so without it being obvious to everyone that there had been something between us. I knew now it was over, whatever the reason had been, and I knew it was for the best - but that did not stop it hurting.

Somehow I ended up walking out to the stables with my sister, father, Lord Lisle, the Viscount and several other guests who had become bored of being indoors and fancied a good ride. The snow had stopped falling, but the world was still a beautiful blanket of white. I wondered if the lake would be frozen over; when we had first discovered it, the previous January when we had moved here, Grace and I had shrieked in delight at the solid ice and how we could slide all over it - although Father had later warned us we were lucky it did not break beneath us.

Remembering being that carefree tugged at my heartstrings, and as I looked at Lord Lisle, striding ahead of me, I wondered if I could be carefree again. It did not feel like he would be one to have fun, to play jokes, to laugh around a dinner table - well, not kindly, in any case.

The horses were waiting, already tacked up, when we arrived - clearly the staff had been pre-warned. I felt, rather than saw, Avery's presence, but I schooled my eyes to focus only on Snowflake. As I'd expected, he was stood next to Shadow, and I heard his voice as he discussed Shadow's welfare and the ride they had been on the day before.

"Let me help you," Lord Lisle said, and I forced a smile on my face as I took a step onto the waiting stool, and allowed him to help me mount the side-saddle. His hands lingered on my waist and I looked down at him, trying to feel some warmth towards this man that I was to marry.

"I have spoken with your Father," he said, and the words made the dread in my stomach feel even heavier. "We have agreed - after our betrothal on Twelfth Night I shall return home, and then a week later we shall be married. Your mother and father will accompany you to Sheffield - it will be more expedient to marry there, and then return to my home afterwards."

I hoped he took my silence for excitement, but he was on his horse before I had managed to get my thoughts together, grinning and motioning for me to ride ahead. I squeezed my boots into Snowflake's flank as the words swirled around my mind. *We've agreed.* And that did not include me, of course. What was the reason for the moved-up wedding date, I wondered, as we slowly walked towards the woods. Were they worried I might flee? I guessed that my questioning of Mother and Father about my prospective husband did not make me look like I was desperate for this marriage - and the sooner it was official, the sooner they did not have to worry about me doing something stupid.

But I'd already done something stupid. The man I *wanted* to marry had heard me saying terrible things - and although I had thought persuading Grace of my disinterest in Avery was for the best, hurting him definitely wasn't. I had hurt someone who actually cared for me, who cared about my feelings, who would ask me before making major, life-altering decisions - and now I would be tied to a man who, it seemed, would never consider my opinion worth seeking.

Perhaps it was what I deserved.

"Avery said the sea is not too far," the Viscount was saying to my father ahead, and my ears pricked at the sound of his name.

"It's probably about an hour's ride," Father said, "If you ride at a decent pace. I'd be happy to accompany you, if you wanted to see it."

The Viscount sighed; "It's too far for these old bones," he said. "In my youth, though... I would have said yes in a heartbeat. The ocean is an incredible sight, don't you think?"

Father nodded, and I wondered when Avery had found the time to ride to the ocean. He had not mentioned it to me, so I presumed it was since we had stopped speaking.

"Perhaps the young people might like to ride out to the sea, however," the Viscount was suggesting, waving his hand in our direction. In a rather uncharitable fashion, I had to stifle a laugh at the thought of Lord Lisle being included in 'the young people'. I thought it might be nice, however, to ride hard and fast and see the ocean - but before I could voice this, he was speaking.

"I do not think the ocean holds much appeal for

us," he said, looking uncertain atop his horse. Had he not tried to make a decision for me, yet again, I might have felt sorry for him at his lack of riding acumen; at how uncomfortable it must be to struggle with a past time that so many enjoyed.

But he had not taken into account my feelings at any step of this so-called courtship, and so I pushed away any pity and decided to rebel.

"I would love to see the sea," I said, and when several of our companions agreed enthusiastically, our course was set. I pictured Avery making this same journey, his strong thighs sat astride Shadow, enjoying every jump and stream the ride offered, marvelling at the winter sunlight on the ocean, the crash of the waves and the endless expanse of water…

As my daydreams threatened to overwhelm me, I could feel Lord Lisle's irritation as he rode behind us. He had decided to come along, although I wasn't sure why; Father and the Viscount had chosen to have a gentle ride round the estate, and he could have remained with them. I guessed he did not want to be included with the older men - despite the fact that he was slightly older than my father - and I tried to calm my irritation enough to build bridges with him. This was my life's path now - I needed to get on board, else I would just be dragged along kicking and screaming.

"Are you looking forward to the play on Twelfth

Night?" I asked him, dropping back a little so our horses were in step with one another. I worried that, at this pace, it would take far longer than an hour to reach the ocean, but did not voice my concerns.

"Your father assures me it will be entertaining," he said, not really answering my question, clearly irritated by my behaviour.

I smiled, hoping it would appease him. "I hope you don't mind this," I said, gesturing to the path in front of us. "I was just excited to see the sea again. I have not found the time to ride out there for a while…"

"Of course, I am happy if you are happy," he said, and while I did not believe his words, he looked a little mollified. "I merely had plans for this afternoon."

"Oh?"

"Just some correspondence. It can wait."

"I'm so pleased," I lied, forcing a smile onto my face.

"And of course, it would not be right for you ladies to go off without an escort."

I did not mention that I had made this journey without a man several times previously; I did not mention that that I would have preferred to make this journey alone.

"Hurry up Isabel!" Grace called from near the front, riding with a speed and joy that I envied. "We want to get there before dark!" Despite not loving riding like I did, she loved an adventure, and her child-like excitement was infectious.

I shrugged apologetically at Lord Lisle, before urging Snowflake on to catch up with the other horses, as she had been desperate to do for the whole ride. The wind whipped through my hair, despite the hood, and I laughed at the freedom I momentarily felt. I heard the hooves of Lord Lisle's mount behind me, but I did not look back to see his displeasure, instead focussing on the path ahead, and on catching up to my sister.

CHAPTER FORTY

Avery

The house was quiet and practically empty as I padded up the stairs, feeling guilty for even being here. If someone caught me, I had no excuse, and so I just hoped no-one would see me. I could only guess which one was her bedchamber from the words I had heard through the window the other day, and thinking of those words made me question my current quest, so I shook them from my mind and pushed open the door.

The room was tidy, with a dress laid out on the dresser that I recognised as one she had worn earlier in the week. Pleased that I had at least found the right room, I took three strides towards the four poster bed and put the wooden engraving under her pillow, before I could change my mind. Things had changed so much between us, but I could not keep hold of the gift I had made for her, and I could not just throw it away.

I took a moment to collect my thoughts, taking

a deep breath as the future I had imagined faded in my mind, and then left, closing the door quietly behind me.

It was time to say goodbye, to try to let go of the hurt and anger and disappointment, and move forwards with my life.

CHAPTER FORTY-ONE
Isabel

It had definitely taken longer than an hour, and the chill wind was penetrating my thick cloak - but the sight of the sea was as glorious as I remembered, and it was like a balm to my aching heart to see it stretched out before me, timeless and endless and unaffected by the dramas in my life.

"It is impressive, don't you think?" I said to Lord Lisle, who had arrived a full twenty minutes after us, looking irritated once more. I knew I should not have left him, but the wild ride had spoken to my soul, and I was powerless to argue.

"It's water," he said, screwing his nose up a little. "I'm not sure I understand why it is worth such a long ride."

"But the beauty of it," I said. "The waves as they swell and crash, the glittering of the sunlight towards the horizon…" His face remained impassive, and I knew I could not persuade him otherwise. "Well, I thank you for accompanying me," I said softly, wondering if the rest of my life was to be filled with lies. Would they drip off my tongue more easily, as I became more practiced?

"Well," he said. "You obviously wanted to come. Perhaps to say goodbye, before moving away."

Tears came to my eyes and I blinked them away furiously, knowing that was a weakness I could not let him see.

The others were dipping their feet in the water, shrieking at the cold as the water splashed their dresses, but I sensed Lord Lisle would not feel that was appropriate, and so I stayed on the beach, Snowflake by my side, enjoying the chance to stretch my legs after the ride.

"Our marriage will unite our families," he suddenly said, and I turned to face him. "And give great honour to your family, and our heirs."

I nodded, not knowing what more was expected of me.

"My sons will be pleased to have a mother again," he said, and once more I nodded. They were not very young, the eldest almost as old as old as I, and I had barely heard him mention them this whole trip. There was no way I could replace their mother, of course - but he seemed to view us as interchangeable, and so once again I held my tongue.

And then he took a step towards me and lowered his lips to mine, and I rooted my feet to the spot, ignoring the urge to run, to hide, to avoid this contact. His breath smelt strongly of something I could not place, and his chin scratched against mine. His tongue thrust into my mouth and I had to stop myself from flinching away. He groaned, pressing his body to mine in a way that did not seem appropriate for an unmarried couple, let alone out in the open, but no-one seemed to be paying us any attention.

And then his hand slipped to my waist, pulling me tighter, and it took everything in my power to not pull away. I could not respond, and I only hoped he took that to be my lack of experience. Of course, my experience was not as limited as he thought - and the blistering kisses that made me want to give everything to Avery were now confined to the past, and could not be compared to this.

Eventually he pulled away, and I tried to smile. He clumsily patted my arm, and I congratulated myself on not saying anything, on not refusing, on not pulling away.

I would be his soon enough, and nothing would be off limits.

Even if the thought made me want to lock myself away and give in to the tears that constantly threatened to overwhelm me.

◆ ◆ ◆

I felt like a clock was ticking permanently in my mind, counting down until I would be betrothed to Lord Lisle. Forty-eight hours until the Twelfth Night celebrations would begin - although I had not asked when they were planning on conducting the betrothal. In the morning? Before the merriment? While everyone else was enjoying the play? No, Father had paid a lot of money to put on a lavish play - he would not want to miss it. If I had to guess, I would have thought it would be before the festivities began, but when we were dressed in our finery. Father did like an element of pomp and formality in everything he did - and this momentous step would be no exception.

We were all tired when we returned from our ride, and I rang for a bath to be run in my bedchamber. It was a luxury, to have the water heated and poured into a tub beside the fire, to languish in its depths and wash away the grime - but one I decided I needed to get through the rest of the day. Avery had once again avoided looking at me as we dismounted, and I had no good reason to speak to him; besides, I was concerned Lord Lisle held some suspicions about us, and as it was clear he did not like Avery, I thought it wise to steer clear of him. I did not want to make life harder for the man who had offered me everything - harder than I already had, at least.

"Sorry for troubling you," I said to Hettie as she directed two pages to bring in the water.

"S'no trouble, Mistress Isabel," she said with that easy smile. Once the tub was full and steaming, Hettie helped me out of my riding clothes and into the water, before closing the door behind her.

I sank my body into the heat, feeling the dirt and grime and misery of the day washing away. I wished I could wash myself of the kiss Lord Lisle had given me, but I knew I would have to grow used to the feel of his lips, and his hands, upon me.

As I sat in the tub, senses and skin tingling, I would not let myself think of Avery. It was a dangerous enough precedent to compare the two when clothed and sensible; in a situation like this, I worried if I let my mind wander to Avery I might never be able to give him up. If I thought of what his fingers could do to my flesh through layers of clothes, the inability to focus that his kisses brought out in me, the desire he awoke in me…

No. I foccussed on using the pressed soap Hettie had left to clean every inch of my body. While some believed that bathing in warm water let illness into the body, I had always enjoyed good health, and had recently discovered the pleasure of soaking in warm water. Never had I needed something to relax my body and take my mind off my woes more than now - and when I stepped out of the tub, clean and shiny with my hair wet down my back, I felt a little better than I had at the end of the ride.

Once I had put on a linen shift, I sat before the fireplace, letting the heat dry my hair and warm my body. Hettie would be here soon to help me dress and to style my hair for dinner, and as I waited I let my mind wander to the enjoyable parts of the day - seeing the ocean, and being able to ride Snowflake at a less serene speed. I wondered if I would be able to take Snowflake with me - not whether my father would allow it, for I was sure he would, but whether Lord Lisle would want his wife to have a horse; to ride regularly. I had a sneaking suspicion he would not.

A quiet knock sounded at the door, and I turned, expecting Hettie, but instead saw Grace at the door. She was already dressed for dinner, but it did not stop her sitting cross-legged on my bed.

"Hello," I said, a question in my voice, but she just smiled. It seemed all was forgiven between us, and for that I was glad.

"I have... a friend," she said, "I won't give up their name, so don't ask. This friend saw a man in your room earlier today."

My eyebrows shot up. "What?" I asked, confusion clouding my mind. "I've been with you all day! Why would a man have been in my bedchamber?"

"Your hair will be terrible to brush if you let it dry all knotted like that," she said, a wicked grin on her face. She was enjoying teasing me, but she was right. I handed her the hair brush and sat in front of her, as we had done when we were little children - although it was usually the other way round. Her dainty hands got to work, brushing through my blonde hair firmly but carefully, and I waited with bated breath for her to continue.

"A very good-looking man, apparently," she said. "With long dark hair, broad shoulders and deep brown eyes…"

"Avery…" I whispered, not able to stop myself. I did not turn to see what that did to the smug look on my sister's face. "I wonder why he was here…"

"Maybe he left something?" she asked, and I shook my head, wincing as I caught it on the hairbrush Grace was wielding.

"He… he heard what I said to you," I whispered, not wanting to own the words that were leaving my mouth. "I hurt him. He… won't even look at me."

The brushing stopped, and I turned to face Grace, tears in my eyes.

"Isabel," she said, her hand on my cheek, and I pressed my face into it and let the tears fall.

"Oh Gracie," I said, for once not being the responsible older sister. "Everything is such a mess."

She stroked my back, and I could feel the warmth of her hand through the thin layer of clothing, calming me a little. "Isabel, you don't have to marry Lord Lisle."

"I do, though! The family…"

"The family will be fine. It won't change anything, Isabel - all it will do is make you miserable. And all the riches and fine marriages and introductions at court aren't worth you spending your life as a miserable wife."

I gasped at her words, not used to seeing my little sister in such an authoritative role.

"But is it not my duty?"

"Well," she said, that grin back on her face. "You know how I feel about duty. Isn't it always amazing that the woman has to be miserable, and sacrifice everything, for duty? Somehow Lord Lisle needs a rich wife, and he gets a pretty young woman and a big dowry. I don't think he's sacrificing anything out of a sense of duty to his family - do you?"

The words she said were shocking, and yet they

lit a fire in me, a fire of hope.

"I don't want to marry him," I said, the only time I said it out loud to anyone except Avery.

"Obviously," she said, and we both laughed, a carefree sound I thought I had forgotten.

"I don't want to break Mother and Father's hearts…"

"They'll heal. They've still got me to marry off."

I grimaced at that, knowing that I had been trying to get a good marriage for her with my own marriage - but realising that she was right. It was not the right path - for either of us. "They might have trouble when it comes to getting you to marry who they think is suitable…" I said with a laugh, and she joined me.

"They have no idea!"

A sudden burst of joy rushed over me at the thought that there was a way out. Even as I realised I had underestimated my sister, I also realised that the feeling of impending doom was calming.

"But…" I faltered, taking hold of my sister's hand. "But Avery agreed. He agreed we should not see each other again, agreed it was for the best. I don't believe he wants to marry me any more."

Grace sighed. "If the way he was looking at you today as we set off to ride is anything to go by, I don't think you have anything to worry about."

"Really?"

She nodded. "But if he's a fool, then you'll find someone else to fall in love with."

"I..." Love? I wasn't totally sure that was what I felt, but now was not the time to discuss it, not with Hettie due any moment. "If I don't marry, I fear Mother and Father will force me to marry Lord Lisle."

Grace screwed up her face, as if she could not bear to think of her parents doing such a thing, but I knew how ambitious they were; I could not be sure they wouldn't resort to underhand tactics.

"You should speak with Avery," she said. "Then - well, we'll cross that bridge if we come to it."

I nodded. "When did you become so wise?" I asked, tapping her nose gently with a smile.

She rolled her eyes; "I always have been. You have just never realised I'm not a child anymore."

And with that she flounced from the room, leaving my heart freer than it had been in days. I lay back on the bed, staring at the curtains above me, and taking long, deep breaths. She was right. As soon as I could, I would go to Avery, I would tell him I was wrong, I would beg him to take me back.

I would not marry Lord Lisle.

I turned, feeling something hard digging into the back of my head, and swept a hand beneath the pillow. My fingers grasped a circle of wood, and when I pulled it out to inspect it, I saw an amazing likeness of Snowflake etched into the wood, the grains almost looking like her markings.

Another knock on the door signalled Hettie, and I shoved it back under my pillow, a smile playing on my lips.

It was a gift from him, surely - and it gave me hope.

❖ ❖ ❖

"Avery?" I whispered into the foreboding darkness that surrounded the stables. "Avery?"

I heard a creak, then his footsteps on the ladder, and then, as my eyes adjusted a little and the dim light of the moon made an appearance, I saw him. His face looked a little drawn, his eyes tired, and I wondered if I had woken him up from a deep sleep.

"Isabel..." he said, pain in his voice, and I hated that I had been the one to cause that anguish. "You shouldn't be here. We said everything that needed to be said..."

I could only just make out his eyes, and he was avoiding looking at me. Was his rejection sincere, or out of some misplaced idea that he was not good enough for me?

"Avery," I said, my voice wavering a little, every fibre of my being wanting to reach out and touch him, to feel his warm skin on this cold night and know everything would be well.

But it wouldn't. Not unless we could be together. Grace was right; this was my path, and I had to follow it. At least, I had to try.

I lowered myself to my knees, seeing confusion in his eyes, and let the tears begin to fall as the words left my mouth. "Avery, will you marry me?"

A gutteral sound came from his throat. "Isabel, what are you doing to me? You know we cannot be married. Tomorrow you are to be betrothed, and your wedding will be before the end of the month. You need to marry someone who will elevate your station - not me."

I reached out then, and was gratified that he did not try to remove his hands from mine. They were just as warm as I remembered, and they gave me the strength to ignore his rejection once again. "I was an idiot. Everything I said, all the ideas I had of how I could turn this on its head and make everyone happy - I can't." I laughed, slightly hysterical at how true the words were. "But Avery, it is I who is not good enough for you. I am not as kind as you, nor as patient as you, nor as good with horses as you. I don't have your wit, or your ability to survive no matter what. But-" My breath hitched, and I wished I could see his face more clearly to gauge his reaction, but my tears and the darkness obscured him. "I love you, Avery. When I go to sleep at night, all I think of is you. When I want to feel safe, all I think of is you. You offered me marriage with no thought for yourself, and I am asking you - begging you - to marry me."

Well. I had done it now; he would either believe me, or he would see me for the desperate woman I had become, and thank his lucky stars we had not run away together.

The silence seemed never-ending, punctuated only by the sound of an owl hooting in flight above us. I remained kneeling, as if in prayer, and waited for some answer, some sign that he had heard my words.

"When should we marry?" His voice sounded unsure, but the words were the ones I wanted to hear - even if there was no declaration of love within them. Love could come later; I knew I loved him, and that was enough for me.

"Now!" I said, my voice barely above a whisper.

"Now?"

"Yes! It was your plan in the first place. Once we are married, they can do nothing. We don't need a church, or a priest - we can do that later. We just need the words, and a witness, and..."

"And to consummate the marriage?"

My cheeks burned liked glowing embers, but I nodded.

CHAPTER FORTY-TWO

Avery

She really meant it. This vision before me wanted me to marry her - was begging me to marry her - and said she loved me.

And I loved her.

It was a feeling I had not known before, and I did not want to speak it before I was sure, but I was almost certain now that these feelings, no matter how quickly they had come upon me, were love.

And she was putting herself in this vulnerable position, telling me all the ways I was wonderful, without a word or a promise from me.

If I felt she were overselling me, I did not say; my decision had been made as though it were written in the stars, and I wanted nothing to get in the way now. No, the quicker we were married, the quicker our future was assured - and there would be so much time for words of love later.

"Can we find a witness, at this hour?" I asked, and I saw a smile break through her tears. Oh how I wanted to kiss them away - but I would control myself, for now.

But not for much longer.

She nodded; "I can wake my sister," she said.

Gently, I pulled on her hands, not wanting to see her kneeling in the snow, and held them as she steadied herself.

"And you're sure?" I asked, needing to know before I committed my heart fully to this woman. "Because there is no undoing this - no matter what King Henry thinks."

She nodded, another tear dropping from her eye; "My heart knows it wants you."

As much as I wanted to control myself, passion overtook, and for a moment I pulled her roughly to me, hoping my lips would convey my feelings where my words did not. It was only brief; we needed to follow through with the plan. But when we pulled apart she looked flushed and breathless and I hoped she had felt how much of myself was truly in that kiss.

She hurried off into the night and I lit a candle, hoping to make myself a little more presentable with the coat she had given me. I combed my fingers through my hair and took several deep, steadying breaths.

It was not long before she hurried back, flanked by her younger sister who was wrapped in a thick cloak. I wondered what Isabel had told her, in order to bring her out of her bed in the middle of the night. The whole truth? She must be very sure of her not to worry she would run to her father and ruin everything. Not for the first time, I wondered what it would have been like to have siblings who survived childhood; someone to watch my back.

"Good evening," I said to her, as though this were the most normal thing in the world, and she smiled back at me as though she were truly happy to be here.

Snowflakes began to fall from the sky once again, softly landing on the existing snow, as well as in Isabel's loose golden waves. I reached out to brush them away, and she smiled like I was giving her the world.

I did not deserve this woman - but I was about to make her mine.

I took her hands in mine, deciding that although it was colder, it was certainly more romantic to marry in the snow than in a stable. Were there certain words that needed to be said? I did not know, and so when she opened her mouth to take the lead I was more than grateful.

"I, Isabel," she said, her voice ringing out like a bell in the silent night. "Take thee Avery to my wedded husband, and there unto I plight my troth."

Perhaps it was not traditional for the woman to say the words first, but nothing about our courtship had been traditional - and it did not bother me a whit.

"I, Avery," I repeated, feeling a comfort from just holding her hands in mine, "Take thee Isabel to my wedded wife, and there unto I plight my troth."

There. It was done. The words were said and, with the exception of the consummation of the marriage, we would be considered wed even by the most holy of priests.

"You should seal it with a kiss," Grace said, a grin on her face, and I remembered her pointing out the kissing bough on the day I had arrived.

In front of me, Isabel shivered a little, and I did not know if it were the cold or the anticipation of this kiss. But Grace was right; such an important moment should be marked. I stepped closer, so our bodies were touching in the snowy night, keeping hold of her hands tightly. I wished I had a ring, or some token to offer her, but I only had my name, and my heart.

Both were hers now.

She tilted her head, snow falling from her hair as she did so, and I could see the warmth of our breath swirling in front of us in the cold night air.

Our lips met with only the slightest pressure, and yet I felt her melt into me. I was at least vaguely aware of her sister watching on, and so I did not deepen the kiss. Instead I held her close, and moved my lips to her forehead, wondering what on earth we would do now.

Her eyes were on me, although when she spoke, it was not directed at me.

"Good night, Gracie. Thank you."

"Are you not-oh." Her sister's eyes widened, but she began to walk back to the house without another word, the crunching of snow beneath her feet slowly fading away.

I let go of her hands and ran my fingers through my hair. Nerves were definitely fluttering in my stomach, although I wasn't sure exactly the reason why.

"You know I sleep in the stables, don't you?" I said, her dismissal of her sister suggesting she planned for us to consummate this marriage now.

"I don't care," she said, biting her bottom lip a little, and I felt undone by those words.

I held out my hand, and led her through the wooden archway.

CHAPTER FORTY-THREE
Isabel

I could not quite believe what I had done. I had said the words that bound me to Avery, and now we would be bound in actions as well as words.

And Mother had not yet managed to talk to me about the marriage bed - although I doubted the stables were what she had imagined. Truly, I did not care about the location - but my nerves were threatening to overwhelm me. I did not know what I was doing, I did not know if it would hurt, I did not even know how to talk to Avery about what we were about to embark on.

He put the candle safely in a holder, leaving enough dim light that we could see our way, and then let me climb the ladder first. I hitched my skirts and tried to calm my breathing as I climbed onto the level where he slept. There was not much there; what looked like a book, although it was hard to see in the dim light, some blankets, a straw mattress and a small leather bag. Hearing the ladder creak under his weight I moved to the side, surprised there was enough height to comfortably stand here.

He sat, without really looking at me, and slowly removed his coat, and then his shoes, until he was sitting with just his lawn shirt and breeches.

And then he turned that smile on, that one that made my heart melt and my head forget every thought that had ever run through it.

"This was not how I expected tonight to end," he said.

"Me neither," I managed to answer, very conscious of how dressed I was and how far away I seemed to be standing from him, despite the space being small.

"Come and sit?" he said, patting the straw mattress next to him, and I swallowed before making my feet move towards him.

It wasn't that I did not want to - I was just so nervous, I couldn't think straight. Well, that and the power of his smiles.

He took my hand, when I had finally sat close enough to him, and brought it to his lips for a searing kiss that made my eyes flutter closed.

"Isabel," he said, in that deep, smooth voice that cut through my fears. "Don't be afraid."

"I don't know what to do," I admitted, pleased the semi-darkness saved me some of my embarrassment.

Some, at least.

"I do," he said. "And we don't have to do anything - not if you're not ready. I know everything has moved so quickly…"

"Do-do you not want to?" I asked, suddenly nervous for a whole host of other reasons.

He laughed. "Should I lie?"

I shook my head.

"Isabel, I've wanted to take you to bed since the moment I first saw you. And now you're my wife, and I can't quite believe that, but yes, I definitely want to."

Wife. It sounded so strange, and yet hearing it on his lips didn't frighten me.

I turned to face him, letting my fingers reach out to touch his beautiful hair, before resting them on his lips.

"Husband," I said, and his smile warmed me even in this chilly barn.

I took a deep breath, and turned away from him, gathering my hair to one side. "Will you unlace me? Please?"

"It would be my pleasure," he said, but instead of his fingers on the ribbons I felt his lips on my neck, and I could not contain the groan of pleasure that escaped my mouth. His touch sent sparks flying through me, a promise of something more.

Every time he loosened a section, he placed a kissed there, and by the time he had reached the base and pulled the corset away from my body, I had almost forgotten my state of undress, thanks to the want he sent coursing through my body.

"You are beautiful," he said, as he pulled me round to face him, and I blushed to realise he had removed his shirt too, so neither of us wore anything above the waist. I reached out, curious, letting my hand rest on the soft skin of his stomach, feeling the muscles that hard work had brought to his body.

"So are you," I said, marvelling at this man before me. His hand moved to my waist, pulling me closer, and as I felt his bare skin against mine I gasped. Longing pooled between my legs and what little I understood of what was to come jumped into action.

His hand moved to my ankle, slowly gliding up my leg until it disappeared between my skirts. It was hard to focus on anything but the sensations he inspired in me, and while a part of me was a little shocked at what was happening, the rest relaxed into the knowledge that he was my husband, and there was nothing prohibited about what was about to happen.

We lay back on the mattress, my heart beating so fast I felt sure he would be able to hear it. There was no rush in the way he moved, and I tried to relax - although that was a battle I was losing.

"It might hurt, a little..." he said, and I nodded. I'd heard that, whispered among the women who were already wives, and although I shied away from any thought of pain, the movement of his hands on the delicate skin of my thighs was enough to distract me from my worries.

"Tell me to stop," he whispered in my ear, dropping a kiss behind my lobe. "If you want me to stop."

I nodded again, not sure I was even capable of forming words, and focused on his face, so close to mine. I could not resist running a hand across the roughness of his stubble, exploring the sinews of his neck as he reached to kiss mine and made me gasp.

I was glad I had worn a simple dress, one which took little to take off and had no smock beneath it. Without my realising, my skirt had been removed, and I put my arms around his neck to hold him closer, needing his warmth as the cool air hit my body.

I had noticed he was still far too clothed, but could not bring myself to comment; thankfully he divested himself of the rest of his garments until he lay next to me, not a stitch of clothing left - and when I saw his full glory, the panic really set it.

Surely, this could not work? My mind was racing, and I wondered if stories of 'a little pain' had been grossly understated.

"Isabel," he said, his voice warm and comforting amidst my panic. He stroked his fingers down my arm and back up my side, making me shiver. "I love you."

It was the first time the words had crossed his lips, and I smiled at the sound of them. I had not been sure of his feelings - of whether this would be a marriage where love needed to bloom later. The thought that he loved me now, before we had even consummated the marriage, made my heart glow.

And then his lips were on mine, and he was hovering above me, and those gentle fingers moved between my legs - and a whole new pleasure that I had never known existed became apparent.

I gasped, then met his gaze, shock and awe on my face. He continued to move them, and as I closed my eyes and gave myself to the shocking feeling building inside me, suddenly whatever was going to happen next was not so daunting.

"Do you trust me?" he asked, a breathy whisper next to my ear, and I nodded.

As he moved between my legs, I closed my eyes in anticipation, already missing the feel of his fingers. And then the pain, a sharp tearing feeling that made me gasp in a completely different way than I had before.

His lips were on mine, and soothing words fell from them, and as he held very still I began to feel the pain calming a little. Knowing that this bound us together made it feel worth the discomfort - and even as I wondered what would happen next, he began to move. Slowly at first, still whispering sweet words in my ear. And both of our breathing became laboured, and words were no longer feasible. The burn was still there, but there was something else, something that I did not understand but that I needed more of. I was too embarrassed to look at him, even though I wanted to see more of that beautiful body, and so I kept my eyes closed as we moved together, and when there were gasps and groans I was not always sure who they came from.

"Isabel…" he said, and then I felt him explode, his breath coming in short spurts and a heat filling me. For just a moment I felt like I could not breathe, with his weight on top of me - but once he rolled away I missed it, and the cold air that came rushing between us was not welcome.

I let my eyes flutter open as I looked at this man who was now my husband, who in everyone's eyes I would now belong to, and felt the same certainty that this decision was right as I had when we had spoken the words before Grace.

He didn't speak, but moved his hand back between my legs, and my eyes widened as his fingers began to move again. Was this normal? I was sure the act was complete, but I could not find the words to question him and the movements felt so heavenly I lost any desire to. Again, that want built, although I did not know what I was seeking.

He watched my face as though it held some great secret, and the intensity of his gaze, of his fingers, of this feeling that I was racing towards, made my eyes close tight shut. And then...

And then I lost all control of my thoughts, my words, my body. It was like something snapped within me, and as my breath mirrored his shallow gasps of before, I felt a warmth of satisfaction flood through me.

When I finally opened my eyes, my body still and my heart racing, he was lying next to me, an arm lazily thrown across my body, a smile on his face.

"What-" I did not even know what question I wanted to ask. What was that? How did he do that? Could we please do that again and again?

His smiled turned to a chuckle, and he pulled me close, dragging a blanket over the two of us. I knew, before we were discovered, we needed to leave this place; no-one was going to be happy about this news, and it was safer for both of us to be far away. But for now I revelled in the feeling of his strong arms around me, of the warmth of his body beneath the rough blanket, of this feeling that surrounded me.

"No turning back now," I said, a shy smile on my face.

"Thank God," he said, and as he pressed his lips to my neck, I felt like nothing could be more perfect than this moment, in the fading light of a candle among the straw.

◆ ◆ ◆

Dear Mother, Father and Grace, I wrote, in the light of the dying fire of my bedroom. Better to include Grace's name - then perhaps they would not find out her part in my marriage.

I am sorry. I know how much you wanted me to marry Lord Lisle, and I know how important it was to the family, but I just could not go through with it. I do not believe we were suited, and I do not believe either of us would have been happy in the marriage.

I am sorry I could not find the words to tell you this in person. I have fallen in love, and I have married, and I am safe with him. Please do not try to follow us; our marriage cannot be annulled.

I blushed at the implication, but knew it needed to be said - else my father would have every man available out on horseback, ready to drag me back.

Know I am happy, and will send word of a contact address when I can. I hope you can find it in your hearts to forgive me, one day. I will miss you all - but I must follow my heart.

Your loving daughter and sister,

Isabel

I did not sign my surname; of course it would now be Peyton, but I didn't want to give them any clues to find us. Of course, once it was noticed Avery was gone too, they would surely grill the Viscount for details - but I was not going to be the one to give them up.

I glanced around the room that had been mine for just over a year, and let a tear drop. I would miss this place, and I would miss my family - but that would have been the case whomever I had married. Now, at least, I knew that I would have a chance at happiness. And as I left the room as silently as possible, packed bag in hand, I did not look back.

❖ ❖ ❖

Sunlight streamed through the windows that did not have curtains, and I blinked, becoming accustomed to my unusual surroundings. The bed was not my own, but it was not uncomfortable, and was not the unusual element.

No, it was the bare arms that encircled my waist. They were new, and altogether delicious. After we had left, taking Snowflake and a few other of my possessions, we had ridden towards the seaside, both sat astride the horse, me settled in between Avery's powerful thighs. Just sitting there had made it hard for me to focus, and as we had ridden in the dark, the light of the moon illuminating the way, I had reflected on the fact that Avery had not commented on the fact that I was riding astride. No judgment, no shock - in fact, it was expected.

We had reached this little inn when we were both in danger of falling asleep while still riding, and were lucky to find they had one small room available, and that we had the coin to pay for it.

And while it had been odd to undress in front of a man, to have him help me take off my dress, for him to kiss me by the light of the candle, when we had curled up in the bed together, nothing had felt more natural.

CHAPTER FORTY-FOUR
Avery

'*A room for my wife and I*'. I hadn't been able to believe I was saying the words, that they were really true, that we had married and consummated the marriage and that this was the reality. Although, it had been hard to forget about consummating the marriage as we rode her horse, nestled together. But when we had reached the inn, exhausted and a little overwhelmed, we had curled up in bed together and fallen asleep as easily as blowing out the candle.

But this morning... this morning I woke up to find her still in my arms, wearing a thin shift, her blonde hair streaming across the pillow. I reached across to run my fingers through it, and was rewarded with a shy smile and a blush rising in her cheeks.

"Good morning," I said, hoping that she was not

feeling any regrets this morning. Legally, it was a little late to turn back - but I supposed her sister was the only witness, and could possibly be persuaded to deny the marriage. Nerves built in my stomach as her eyes roamed my face, silently - and I wondered why my head had to jump to the worst conclusion, when I held her here in my arms, the winter sunlight bathing us in a hazy glow.

She cleared her throat then, and smiled. "Good morning," she said, and the fact that she wasn't running from the room made my panic subside a little. We needed to plan, of course - we needed to decide where in this country we wanted to live, and how we were going to find a home, and when we wanted to get the church to bless our union. Before we had children, I supposed - which, I realised with a jolt, could have been created last night.

But this morning I wanted to make sure she was content, and I let my fingers trail from her hair, down her cheek, ghosting along her collar bone and down the side of her thinly-clothed breast.

She gasped, letting her head roll back into the pillow, and I could not help but smile.

"Are you... in pain, from yesterday?" I asked her, not knowing the effects of the loss of her innocence - especially combined with a long horse ride.

She blushed, and shook her head. "I think-" She was whispering, and I moved my head closer to hear her. "I think it will be all the more wonderful in a bed," she said, and I laughed.

"I think so too." And then the time for words was over, and my lips were on hers, and a groan escaped my lips as her fingers threaded through my hair, pulling me closer. We had gone to bed wearing little, and so there was little in our way as we ached to press bare flesh against bare flesh. She responded to me in a way I wouldn't have been able to imagine, and as I pressed my lips to the hollow of her throat, I felt her fingertips stroking up my back.

"Avery..." she whispered, and I thrilled at the sound of my name on her lips.

"Isabel," I responded, and as we joined together I gasped at the feeling of completeness. It wasn't just the delicious feeling of being with her, or the build towards release I could already feel - it was something more. Something warm and promising, which made the whole future seem to glow with possibilities.

CHAPTER FORTY-FIVE

Isabel

It was so much less daunting this time, and as he entered me I grasped his back, desperate to feel closer to him. This man who had given me a future I thought was impossible, who was willing to bet everything he had planned on *us* - this man that I had grown to love. We moved together, and I tried to follow his lead, learning quickly what felt good, what made him groan in that delicious way that made me feel like I could do anything.

Then that feeling began to build, the one that had made me feel like the whole world was shattering around me, and as he continued to move I had to still my hips just to focus on the feelings that were threatening to overwhelm me. My breath turned to gasps, and with a shout I dug my fingers into Avery's tight muscles, pulling him even tighter as the exquisite pleasure washed over me, and as the haze of ecstasy began to clear in my mind, I saw pleasure wash over his face too.

Panting, we lay next to one another, his arm brushing up against mine, and for a few moments we did nothing but listen to the sound of our hearts hammering and our heavy breathing.

Then he turned to me, the most beautiful smile on his face, and I found my lips mirroring his.

"I love you," he said, more confidently this time, and I felt my heart soar. Yes, we would face challenges. Yes, my life would be wildly different than anything I'd ever known. But if I could spend my nights in bed with this beautiful man, feeling the joy he could make me feel, knowing he loved me and I loved him - I was sure everything would be fine.

"I love you," I repeated, pressing my lips to his and nestling my head into the crook of his arm.

CHAPTER FORTY-SIX

Avery

I held her close, feeling both of our heartbeats thrumming together, and closed my eyes as our beautiful future played in my mind. I would have a wife to come home to, a family to love, a home to call my own.

What a perfect image.

CHAPTER FORTY-SEVEN
Epilogue - Grace

"I know you're upset," I said, placing my hand on my father's arm and speaking in calming tones. "But she will be happy."

"How do you know that?" he asked, and I panicked. Isabel had very carefully not implicated me in the escape - and yet now, here I was, admitting all.

Well, maybe not quite all.

"We spoke of how upset she was to marry Lord Lisle," I said carefully. "And I know she will be happier with…someone else."

"The Viscount says his groom is gone," Mother said, sashaying into the room and taking a seat, her face a little grey. "He'd left a note to say he had fallen in love, and was sorry."

"She's married... she's married a groom?" Father's voice was pained, and I tried to soothe him.

"Just focus on the happiness part. Remember, you married Mother for love - would it have mattered to you if she were a scullery maid?"

He looked up, his eyes meeting with his wife's, and even after all these years, even with the heartbreak their daughter's elopement had caused, he knew the answer.

"No," he murmured. "No, it would not have mattered to me."

I crossed my arms triumphantly. I would get my point across - and, if I had my way, secure Isabel and Avery the dowry to boot.

◆ ◆ ◆

It was two weeks later when I finally raised the topic. A letter had arrived that morning from Isabel, letting me know she was safe and happy and that they had rented a little cottage. No clues were given to her whereabouts, but I knew that was just to avoid any scene with our parents.

It had been a quiet two weeks, after the excitement and clamour of Christmas. The guests - including a disgruntled Lord Lisle and an irritated Viscount - had left, and everyone had gone back to work. The decorations were gone, and I was able to spend my days painting, and reading, and not worrying about whom I might offend.

It gave me time to think. This Christmas had made me realise just how easily a man could decide the whole course of a woman's life, without even asking her - and despite the fact that no prospective husband had been mentioned for me yet, I planned to be ready when it was. I was not going to sleepwalk into a marriage that I did not want, I was adamant about that - but, hopefully, I would not have to resort to elopement like Isabel.

"Good morning, Father," I said, entering the library with a quiet knock. His smile was strained, but it was there, and I settled myself on the chair opposite him.

"Do you have a moment?" I asked, and he nodded, closing the book in front of him. I had wondered so many times since Isabel had woken me in the middle of the night to witness her marriage, whether they truly would have made her go through with a marriage she dreaded. I liked to think they would have reconsidered… but I could not be sure.

"I have heard from Isabel," I said, seeing his eyes widen at her name. "I don't know where she is, but she says she is happy, and safe."

He swallowed, looking like he wanted to rant

and rail, but settled for a stiff nod. "Well. I'm glad she's safe."

"I... I should not want to never see her again," I said, and it took a few moments for the silence to build to an uncomfortable level, where he felt forced to answer.

"Well. I'm sure... once the dust settles... perhaps..."

"But of course, it would not be acceptable for me to spend time with someone of little means, if I am planning to marry well," I said, putting a haughtiness in my voice that I had been practicing. I was rewarded with a nod from Father, and stifled my grin at how easily this was moving along. "But if she were a yeoman farmer's wife..."

"But she is not, is she?"

"But she could be. Perhaps if she had her dowry..."

He sighed, and for a moment I thought I had lost him as I tried to lead him down my carefully planned path.

"Very well," he said, and I could not contain my smile. "I shall consider it. She needs some time to think about her actions - but I will consider sending them her dowry."

"I think that is an excellent plan, Father," I said,

standing to leave.

"Don't you dare get any ideas though, young lady," he said, suddenly stern. "No elopement. No fraternising with anyone inappropriate. We will find you a husband and you will be well-married, as your sister ought to have been."

"Of course, Father," I said, skipping from the room.

If all went to plan, he would think he had chosen my husband - and I would marry someone I truly loved.

WANT MORE?

Can't get enough of Tudor romance? Get a free short story set in 'The Hearts of Tudor England world' here: https://tinyurl.com/restoremyheart

Read on for a sneak peak at book 4 in 'The Hearts of Tudor England' series: Saving Grace's Heart.

SAVING GRACE'S HEART

The simple lawn shirt and hose were a little big on me, but I managed to do them up tightly enough so they would not fall to the floor. My hair was a little more challenging; long, dark, and often worn loose thanks to my unmarried status, it would immediately give me away as being a girl, and today I did not want anyone to know that. Thankfully, the woollen cap I had procured was large enough that I could stuff my hair beneath it, and once I added a cloak I thought I could pass for a tall lad - as long as no-one looked too closely.

A grin spread across my face as I checked myself in the looking glass, then cocked my head slightly to listen for any signs of movement in the room adjoining mine. We had been living at Court for four weeks now, and for a merchant family it was a very great honour. But as exciting as the balls and feasts and jousts were, I needed to experience London from the other side - and so today, I was going to do just that.

It had taken several years, but at eighteen years old I felt fairly proficient in getting my own way. Many times, my father had tried to betroth me to a young man of his choosing, and every time I had managed to persuade him that it was not the right time; that he was not the right man.

So when I had decided I wanted to watch a play, being shown in the courtyard of a local inn, it wasn't a question of whether I would be allowed - but how I was going to manage it.

I made my way down the corridor as quietly as I could, but no-one seemed to notice me leaving. And once I was out in the fresh air, no-one cared - I was just another lad, busy working at the Court of Henry VIII.

The freedom gave me a spring in my step, and I took a deep breath, letting the fresh February air fill my lungs. The day was cold but dry, and I revelled in the joy of slipping through the crowd unnoticed. No-one was looking at the dress I wore, or discussing whom I might marry, or gossiping about how my family had made their way in the world.

No - they ignored me. And while I was very grateful for the privileges my father's riches brought, it was very pleasant to be a nobody - just for a little while.

I walked out of the boundaries of the castle, knowing my decision to dress as a boy had been the right one - no-one challenged me, or suggested I should be accompanied. When had I last been alone like this? I could not remember a time when my mother, or a maid, had not been at my side.

When I reached the rowdy inn, I paused; was this a mistake? As much as I wanted to experience real London life, it was a little daunting.

"The play's about to start!" the woman at the doorway shouted, and I squared my shoulders and hurried over, paying the penny entrance and crowding into the courtyard, where everyone faced a makeshift stage.

The smell was not pleasant - a mix of sweat and weak beer - but as soon as the actors came on stage, I was entranced. I knew the tale of Robin Hood well, but that did not stop me hanging on every word. The actors wore simple clothes, but their roles were clear as they spoke words which painted a picture more intricate than one I had ever painted with my watercolours.

"I will not rest until I hang that bandit!" the Sheriff

of Nottingham shouted, as Robin leapt past him and straight into the audience. We shrieked, trying to get out of their way, and in the rush of people I found myself knocked to the floor, my cap flying off into the crowd.

Fear shot through my body; what would my parents do if I were found here, alone, dressed as a boy? I scrambled across the floor, avoiding dirty boots and questionable spillages as best I could, reaching my fingers as far as they would stretch for the cap. If I could just get it back on my head before anyone noticed…

And then a hand clenched around the grey wool, and my heart stopped.

I did not look up, not wanting to risk someone recognising me. Instead I clambered to my feet, keeping my eyes on the floor, and holding out my hand for the much-needed cap.

"Please," I said, trying to keep my voice deep, although with long dark hair falling around my shoulders, there wasn't much point in the pretense.

There was a chuckle, and then I felt the coarse material of the hat pushed into my hand. I shoved it on my head, without bothering to hide my hair completely, muttered a word of thanks and then darted from the courtyard. As much as I would have loved to have seen the end of the play, there had been too much risk already, and I waited until I was a decent way from the building before stopping to catch my breath and sort my hair.

My heart was thundering like a horse's hooves, and I could feel my cheeks flaming red. That had been close - but oh, it had been worth it. The excitement rushing through my veins was something I would not soon forget - and seeing a play performed with such an excited audience was an experience I was glad to have.

For now, though, I needed to return to the palace, prepare for the feast the following night, and pretend I had spent the day sewing...

Continue reading: mybook.to/tudorhearts4

AFTERWORD

Thank you so much for reading 'Misrule My Heart'. This story has a special place in my heart because I love Christmas (I have written several Christmas novels!) and researching Tudor Christmas traditions was so much fun!

I am not a historian, simply an author who loves romance and the Tudor era, so please forgive any errors. I hope I have given a flavour of the Tudor times while sharing Isabel and Avery's love story!

I would love to read your reviews of this novel once you finish - they really do make a difference, if you want to get in touch, you can email me at rebeccapaulinyi@gmail.com or visit my website rebeccapaulinyi.comm

Thanks again for spending time in the Hearts of Tudor England world. There are 5 other books in the series for you to enjoy!

BOOKS IN THIS SERIES

The Hearts of Tudor England

Six enchanting stories of love, loss and laughter, set in the Tudor Era.

The Love Of A Lord

When grieving hearts find each other, can love overcome secrets, vows and society's expectations?

Compelled to uncover the secret surrounding her mother's death, Annelise Edwards unexpectedly finds herself the guest of the handsome Lord Gifford.

Lord Nicholas Gifford has no interest in women after being jilted by his betrothed, but he cannot ignore his sense of duty when a mysterious woman appears on his doorstep during a terrible storm and falls ill.

As they wait for the storm and Annelise's fever to pass, they are forced to share the grief that is weighing on both their hearts. And when Nicholas becomes more involved in Annelise's efforts to piece together her mother's past, it becomes increasingly difficult to deny their blooming attraction.

Will Nicholas give up the lonely life he has become accustomed to? And will it even matter once he finds out Annelise's mother was nothing but their maid?

If you like your rags to riches romance mixed with Tudor drama, you'll love this heart-warming first novel in the touching The Hearts of Tudor England series.

The Love of a Lord is book one in The Hearts of Tudor England series, and can be read as a standalone novel.

Can't Let My Heart Fall

When a marriage is arranged for Alice and Christopher, love was never part of the bargain.

Alice Page long ago swore she would never fall in love. After watching her father's heartbreak at the death of her mother, and Queen Katherine's pain at her husband's philandering, it just doesn't seem worth the pain.

Marriage to Christopher Danley, however, makes keeping that solemn vow to herself somewhat difficult. In the daytime she can keep her distance, but at night she realises she has never felt closer to another human before.

Lord Christopher 'Kit' Danley knows he will be an Earl one day, but he plans to spend every moment of the time before that happens travelling the seas and discovering new lands. When his father delivers an ultimatum, marriage is the only option – but never did he imagine he would find marriage as enjoyable as he does with Lady Alice.

With Alice panicking at realising her heart may be lost to the handsome Kit Danley, and Kit called away on the King's business, can love flourish in this marriage of convenience?

Can't Let My Heart Fall is book two in The Hearts of Tudor England series, and can be read as a stand-alone novel.

Misrule My Heart

When Isabel realises over the Twelve Days of Christmas that she cannot marry the man she is required to, will she follow her family's wishes or her heart's desires?

Isabel Radcliffe knows she must marry well. As the daughter of a merchant who has risen at court, many opportunities are within her grasp - and marrying a Lord is one of them.

When her father hosts nobility over the Twelve Days of Christmas, she knows she will meet the man he wishes her to marry, and begin the life that has been laid out before her.

What she does not expect is for him to be quite so old or quite so unpleasant...

Suddenly, the duty binding her to such a life-changing decision feels like too much of a sacrifice. And when her head and heart are turned by the dashing and daring stable lad Avery, she questions whether she can follow through with her father's wishes.

A tale of love, duty and the magic of Christmas, with a dose of Tudor drama.

Misrule My Heart is book three in 'The Hearts of Tudor England' series, and can be read as a stand-alone novel.

Saving Grace's Heart

Since witnessing her sister's romantic elopement,

Grace Radcliffe has been determined to choose her own husband.

And while finding excuses not to marry every man her father has put in her path has worked so far, she knows time is not on her side - and so she sets her sights on the handsome Duke of Lincoln, planning to ensure they are a good match before letting her father seal the deal.

When Harry, the dashing new Duke of Leicester, is put in her path instead, she knows there must be something wrong with him - for her father has never picked well in the past.

But when he helps her in her hour of greatest need, she begins to question that judgement.

Can Grace find the route to true love? Or will her free-spirited ways lead her into a loveless marriage?

Saving Grace's Heart is Book Three in 'The Hearts of Tudor England' Series, and can be read as a standalone novel.

Learning To Love Once More

A widowed Earl, a lonely governess, and a whole lot of heartbreak.

James Trant, Earl of Essex, has never known an all-consuming love - but after losing his wife to the perils of childbirth, he resolved not to suffer that pain again.

Fed up of being a burden on her Aunt and Uncle, orphaned Catherine Watt decides being a governess will fill the loneliness in her soul and provide her with a modicum of independence. What she is not expecting is to fall in love with the Earl she is working for.

When James realises he and the children need Catherine in order to flourish, he offers marriage - but in name only. There will be no more children, he is resolute about that.

As Catherine falls deeper and deeper in love with the damaged Earl, can she persuade him that love is worth risking your heart for?

Learning to Love Once More is Book Five in 'The Hearts of Tudor England' series, and can be read as a standalone novel.

An Innocent Heart

On the same day as Henry VIII's second daughter is born, Elizabeth Beaufort makes her way into the world. Inspired by the way the Princess lives her life, she vows to live as a maid - no love, no marriage, no children.

But as the Tudor dynasty sends lives in England reeling, can Bessie Beaufort's heart remain caged?

Edward Ferrers has always known he will marry and carry on his father's merchant business. In fact, such a marriage has been lined up for him for several years - until a chance meeting at the Tudor Court sends his heart racing for Bessie Beaufort.

In a time of courtly love, female purity and religious upset, can Edward persuade Bessie that their love is worth fighting for?

An Innocent Heart is Book Six in 'The Hearts of Tudor England' series, and can be read as a standalone novel.

BOOKS BY THIS AUTHOR

The Worst Christmas Ever?

Can the magic of the Christmas season be rediscovered in a small Devon town?

When Shirley 'Lee' Jones returns home from an awful day at the office, the last thing she expects to find is her husband in bed with another woman. Six weeks until Christmas, and Lee finds the life she had so carefully planned has been utterly decimated.

Hurt, angry and confused, Lee makes a whirlwind decision to drive her problems away and ends up in Totnes, an eccentric town in the heart of Devon. As Christmas approaches, Lee tries to figure out what path her life will follow now, as she looks at it from the perspective of a soon-to-be 31-year-old divorcée.

Can she ever return to her normal life? Or is a new

reality - and a new man - on the horizon?

Finding herself and flirting with the handsome local police officer might just make this the best Christmas ever.

Lawyers And Lattes

A new home, a new man, and a new career are all great - but do they always lead to happily-ever-after?

Shirley 'Lee' Jones has made some spontaneous and sometimes questionable decisions since the breakup of her marriage, but deciding to remain in the quirky town of Totnes has got to be the biggest decision so far. Now Lee has a new business, gorgeous man, and friends keeping life interesting. But when questions of law crop up in her life again, she finds herself yearning for the career and the life plan she gave up when she left everything behind.

And when unexpected news tests her relationship, her resolve, and everything tying her to her life, Lee must decide between the person she is and the person she wants to become.

Sometimes decisions about life, law, and love all reside in grey areas. Will Lee's newfound happiness in Devon be short-lived? Or could her new life give her the chance to have everything she's ever wanted?

Feeling The Fireworks

Can Beth rekindle her passion for life and love in picturesque Dartmouth?

When Beth Davis made a whirlwind decision to move to picturesque Dartmouth to shake up her repetitive life, the last thing she expected to find was a passion in life - or a man who could make her feel fireworks.

A change in home and job seems like exactly what Beth needs to blow away the cobwebs that have been forming around her dead-end job. With little money to her name and no real plan, Beth needs to make things work, fast - without relying on her big sister Lee to bail her out.

When she meets the handsome, mysterious Caspian in a daring late-night swim, she instantly feels fireworks that she had long forgotten. Can Dartmouth - and Caspian - reawaken her passion for life and love?

'Feeling the Fireworks' is Book 3 in the South West Series but can be read as a standalone novel. Fall in love with Devon today.

The Best Christmas Ever

A Devon wedding with the magic of Christmas and a dose of small town charm - and the potential for a lot of family drama.

Lee Davis is about to marry the man of her dreams - and at her favourite time of year. But she's finding it hard to feel the magic of Christmas or the excitement about her wedding as a face from her past reappears and worries about her second time down the aisle surface.

James Knight thought he had everything - the woman he was destined to be with, an adorable daughter and a happy life in the countryside. But with his wife-to-be seeming more and more distant, is he doomed to be jilted at the alter again?

Beth Davis is pretty sure she's lost her heart to handsome, brooding Caspian - but he's moved away to Edinburgh, and their fiery romance seems to have been stopped before it had truly started.

Caspian Blackwell wants to be excited about his promotion and moving to an vibrant new city - but his heart is very much back in Dartmouth.

Can a festive Devon wedding make this the Best Christmas Ever?

Trouble In Tartan

Beth Davis didn't plan on falling in love when she moved to Dartmouth - she just wanted to feel some fireworks. The problem is, she's pretty sure that is exactly what is happening - but the object of her affections is living 600 miles away in Edinburgh. As she tries to start a career as an author, downs a few too many glasses of wine and attempts to make ends meet, keeping a long-distance relationship alive proves more and more challenging.

Caspian Blackwell has never let his heart make big decisions - but he's sorely tempted when the distance between them begins to cause problems in his relationship with Beth. When he decides he wants all or nothing, can he really put this new relationship before his career? Or will he end up exactly where he always feared he would: heartbroken?

A tale of love, longing and a relationship stretched between coastal England and Scotland.

Summer Of Sunshine

A summer holiday can wash up a whole host of family dramas...

Lee Knight wants to relax on a summer holiday

away with her husband, sister and brother-in-law. But her desire for another baby is not making it easy to unwind.

James Knight hates to see his wife upset, and hopes a trip away will make her troubles lessen. But with concerns about his father's health, he's finding it hard to be there for her as much as she really needs.

Beth Blackwell is sick to death of everyone asking her two questions: when is her next book coming out, and when is she going to have a baby. The first is proving more difficult than she expected, and the second - well, she's not sure whether that's the way she wants her life to go.

Caspian Blackwell is enjoying life as a newlywed in Edinburgh - although in his heart, he's missing living in Devon. A spate of redundancies at work has him pondering his future - but he worries his new wife's heart is engaged elsewhere when she becomes increasingly distant.

Can sun, sea and sand send the two couples back into more harmonious waters?

Printed in Great Britain
by Amazon